THE
SCOUR

THE SCOUR

RICHARD SWAN

GdM

THE SCOUR

Acquiring Editor: Adrian Collins
Copy Editor: Ed Crocker
Cover Artist: René Aigner
Map: Jack Shepherd
Cover Design and Interior Layout: STK•Kreations

Hardcover ISBN: 978-1-923459-02-1
Trade paperback ISBN: 978-1-923459-03-8
eBook ISBN: 978-0-6486635-5-3
Worldwide Rights

First Edition, 2025

Published by Grimdark Magazine
Cannon Hill, QLD, 4170
www.grimdarkmagazine.com

THE MERIDIAN OCEAN
Gdansburg
Abbey
Gaol
Harbour Wall
Physician
Wharf
Lighthouse
The Brass Wyvern
SALTMARSH
BANIS
LEYENSWA
DENHOL
GROZOD
GDANSBURG
ANNHOL
Haugen High-way (Under Const
GRALLSTEIN
The Grozodan Peninsula
AND THE PROVINCES THEREIN
as subjugated and absorbed by
the Sovan Empire
DURING THE REIGN OF HIS MOST EXCELLENT MAJESTY
Of the House of Haugenate
ANNO 36 IMPERII SOVI
TI

TOLSBURG
GALEN'S VALE
VASAYA
JÄGELAND
TOLLISH MARCHES
HAUNERSHEIM
River Gale
GRESCH
GUELICH
SCHWANSTADT
Imperial Relay (Completed Haugen Highway)
KOLSBURG
WALDERSTADT
VENLAND
ANNISGEN
River Gale
PORT WESTENHOLTZ
RAHN STRAITS
e Grall Sea
SEPTENTRIO
OCCIDENS
NORT
WEST
OST

I
GDANSBURG

"However valid the resentments and antipathies of the Imperial subjugate, his ready obedience is yours by right. Be compassionate but robust, and take a firm hand to any obfuscation and noncompliance."

—From Caterhauser's *The Sovan Criminal Code: Advice to Practitioners*

"SOME INTERESTING MORSELS about Gdansburg," Bressinger said as he sat down at the table with two charged tankards of marsh ale.

"Oh?"

"Mm. One thing for each of your legal and arcane sensibilities."

"Who told you about my sensibilities?" Vonvalt said, and saw off several large swallows of the lukewarm ale. They were sitting in a crossroads inn twenty miles from Grozoda's Meridian Ocean coast, and the place was hot and loud and lousy with traders.

"Which one would you like to hear first?"

"I will listen to anything except you complain about your urethra."

"By Nema, it burns."

"Dubine: I can't have this conversation again."

"I think it was that whore in Grallstein—"

"What were the two morsels?"

Bressinger leant forward conspiratorially, pausing briefly to rearrange the component parts of his groin. "Apparently the lighthouse in Gdansburg is haunted."

Vonvalt groaned, waving him off. "Rot. What's the other one?"

Bressinger sat back, only slightly put out. "I thought you'd find that interesting."

"And I am happy to tell you that you were wrong. What was the second thing?"

"Talk is that the locals have arrested a Justice."

Vonvalt's eyes widened. "*What*?"

"Just that."

"They have arrested a Justice? An Imperial Justice?"

"Is there any other kind?"

"Where? When?"

"Gdansburg," Bressinger said patiently. "Recently. As recently as yesterday."

"Who told you this?" Vonvalt asked, searching about the inn. The common room was a cramped space, filled with tables and traders. The beams of the ceiling were low and the air was thick with pipe smoke and body odour. Late afternoon sunlight slanted through the west-facing windows.

Bressinger looked around as well. "Can't see him now. Just some bloke. He was hardly out to lead me on. I didn't pay him anything."

Vonvalt clacked his tongue. "Most troubling," he said after a long while. "Most vexing."

"Aye, well," Bressinger said. "You can drink your fill of it tomorrow.

And be troubled, and be vexed, then."

"It is a long way still. We shall leave before dawn."

Bressinger groaned. "I should not have said anything."

"No. I'm glad you brought this to my attention. This is an extremely serious matter."

Bressinger rolled his eyes. "Waking me before dawn is an extremely serious matter."

"No whoring tonight."

"I don't think I should anyway. Not with my ur—"

"Yes, yes."

IN SPITE OF the lingering autumnal warmth, it was chilly and damp in the predawn gloom. They paid the ostler double for the early start, and soon they were saddled up on their horses, with their donkey—upon whom Vonvalt had bestowed the name 'the Duke of Brondsey', on account of both man and beast being obstinate cunts—in tow. It was by virtue of the mule that they travelled slowly, obliged as they were to transport all of Vonvalt's legal accoutrements.

The roads in this part of Grozoda were of poor quality and ill-maintained. Once the Sovan Legions had calcified their grip on the province's abutting Venland and Denholtz—the latter territory absorbed five years previously, the former only one—the plan was to extend the Haugen High-Way all the way to the very tip of the continent. But for now, they were forced to navigate roads of compacted earth, and more often travel across open country.

"You know this area, do you?" Vonvalt asked Bressinger as the sun rose on the Grozodan countryside. This was an expansive, open place, little of it cultivated: huge empty wildflower meadows, scrubby, rocky outcrops, the odd hamlet of dusty, whitewashed adobe nestled in the crooks of streams and at the nexus of small farms. Further east, in the shadow of Annholt, there had been vineyards, too, miles and miles of them. But out here on the peninsula, the countryside and the people were a little rougher.

"Not really," Bressinger said, looking around. "Annholt was big enough for us."

Vonvalt wisely let the conversation rest; the provincial capital, and what it represented, was a source of profound grief for his taskman.

On they went. Vonvalt was troubled by the rumour of the arrest of an Imperial Justice, but could not bring himself to get as exercised about it as he felt he should. The day was warm and pleasant, there was no one about, and the meadows buzzed with bees and the sky trilled with black starlings. And even though he was travelling down the peninsula in his capacity as a Sovan lawkeeper, with the great burden of labour that entailed, there were colder, grimmer, more dangerous parts of the Empire in which to do it.

They rested the horses and mule at midday, and stretched their legs in the shade of a cypress tree. Bressinger fished out a bottle of cheap red from the Duke of Brondsey's cart, and some food, and they enjoyed a ploughman's lunch through the worst of the day's heat. In fact, so unexpectedly pleasant was the journey, and so far did his thoughts wander, that by the time they smelt the ocean's brine Vonvalt had forgotten about the matter of the arrested Justice entirely.

"By Nema," Bressinger said as they approached the outer environs of Gdansburg. "Is there even anybody here?"

Vonvalt looked ahead. The town was spread along several miles of coastline, and had at its westernmost apex a low headland upon which was set the—allegedly haunted—lighthouse. That in itself was part of a broader fastness that had undoubtedly once been the seat of the local lord; but even from their distance, Vonvalt could see that the place had fallen into disrepair, and was clearly abandoned. In fact, the same could be said for much of the town. Gdansburg bore the five-year-old scars of the Reichskrieg, with the outermost parts reduced to overgrown rubble. There was a tangible quietness to the place.

Still, their arrival drew what little attention there was to be drawn.

"Something tells me they are not accustomed to receiving visitors," Bressinger said.

"I daresay you are right."

They had come upon what was the main thoroughfare, a surprisingly broad, paved road that Vonvalt would once have associated with trading towns. But there was no sign of any ships, even though the remains of a harbour lay to the north of the lighthouse. To the south, the headland slowly sloped down until it gave way to an enormous saltmarsh lousy with avocets and a single, lonely harrier.

"Excuse me," Vonvalt said, casting an eye over the main street. It was fronted by a number of shops with no obvious guild closures, as well as sturdy brick and timber townhouses. There was no question that this had once been a place of wealth.

"Yeah?" one of the locals asked, a blonde headed, blonde bearded man who looked very out of place in Grozoda.

"I'd like to speak to the sheriff, please."

"He's dead."

Vonvalt exchanged a brief glance with Bressinger. "Is there a mayor? Or alderman?"

The man spat on to the cobbles. "No."

"Hey!" Bressinger snapped, placing his hand on the hilt of his side sword. "We're obviously looking for the person in fucking charge, so turn your mind to it!"

Even then, the fellow could not be roused to answer quickly. He turned, and pointed to what looked like a Neman abbey that lay on another, lesser headland bookending the old harbour.

"Matria Klement," he said. "She has taken the reins of local government."

"And what is this I hear about a Justice being arrested?" Vonvalt asked, struggling to keep the anger from his voice, for the man's intractability was irritating him greatly.

He shook his head, and latterly his hands. "Oh no. I'm not getting involved in that," he said, and bustled off.

They watched him go.

"What accent was that?" Vonvalt asked after a while.

"Honestly, I'm not sure."

Vonvalt sighed, and looked out across the vast grey ocean. It was getting late in the afternoon, and the clouds were drawing in.

"Come on then," he said eventually. "Let's see what this matria has to say for herself."

VONVALT, AS AN Imperial Justice, was rarely a welcome sight anywhere, but this was especially true in recently subjugated provinces. Justices, after all, were the embodiment of Sovan legal authority, able to arrest, trial, imprison, and execute anyone within the bounds of the Empire. And whilst that in itself was reason enough to be fearful of anybody, he also had several magickal powers with which to enforce those laws—powers which invited mistrust and superstition.

Nowhere was this mistrust more evident than in the Empire's temples and klosters. It was from the Nemans, after all, that the magicks had been taken.

"Plucked from their hands like a toy from a child," Vonvalt murmured as they were reluctantly bade entry into the abbey.

"What?" Bressinger asked, scratching his balls.

"Never mind."

They were led to the matria's office, a well-appointed chamber which overlooked the Meridian Ocean through a bay window of glass and lead lattice. She looked up, her expression curdling as she recognised Vonvalt from his finery and medallion of office.

"Come to take the Justice away have you?" she rasped. She was a tough, rangy woman, sixty if she was a day, with a tangled bird's nest of grey hair and pale, wrinkled skin. She was the kind of person whom Nema would have to physically drag off the mortal coil, kicking and screaming.

"Come to see that justice is done," Vonvalt corrected mildly.

"Oh, he'll be done all right. What is it that you want? News can't have travelled that quickly."

"May we sit?"

"If you must."

They sat.

"And who exactly are you two?"

"My name is Justice Sir Konrad Vonvalt, of the Imperial Magistratum. This is my taskman, Dubine Bressinger."

"Uh huh."

There was a pause.

"And who are you, madam?"

"The matria."

"I'd got that far."

She sighed, and folded her arms. "Radmila Klement."

"I am pleased to make your acquaintance."

"I am not pleased to make yours. What do you want?"

"I am on my circuit, madam. I am here to speak to the townsfolk. Hear their legal complaints. Adjudge, fine, and punish accordingly."

"Well. There's nothing that needs doing here. So why don't you fuck off up the coast?"

Bressinger brandished his finger. "Now see here you miserable old hag—"

"It's all right, Dubine," Vonvalt said, holding out a hand. "Why don't you see if you can find a physician."

Bressinger shrugged, and left.

"You got him well-trained," Klement said.

"Mister Bressinger is a loyal and highly competent lawkeeper and officer of the Crown, and the finest swordsman this side of Sova."

"How lovely for him."

Vonvalt reclined in his chair, and examined the woman in front of him. "You are exceptionally rude."

"And you are taking up my time."

"I am entitled to as much of it as I like," Vonvalt replied. She gave him a venomous look, but did not rejoin. "I heard a rumour on the way here."

"Is that so?"

"That you have detained a Justice."

"We have."

"On what charge?"

"Murder."

Vonvalt's eyes widened slightly. "Indeed?"

"Indeed."

"You have evidence?"

"We have all the evidence we need."

"I have been a Justice for nearly fifteen years now, Matria. Do you know what I have learned in that time?"

"A great many things, I should imagine."

"People who claim to have 'all the evidence they need' tend to have no evidence whatever."

Her expression curdled further. "The matter is out of your hands."

"Nothing could be further from the truth."

She huffed about her desk, unused, no doubt, to having her authority challenged in this place.

"Where is he being kept?"

"That's none of your—"

"Where is he being kept?" Vonvalt asked again, this time using the Emperor's Voice.

The room darkened, and the matria jolted as though she had been punched in the nose. Her throat and mouth worked against her brain, until eventually she gasped out, "...town... gaol."

Vonvalt regarded her as she clutched her habit where her heart squirmed arrhythmically. The Voice—the arcane ability of a Justice to compel a person to speak the truth—worked on almost everybody. But it had taken her a little too long to yield up the answer for his liking, which meant she was somewhat familiar with the power. Those anticipating it, even laypeople, could go some way to frustrating it.

"You know of the Voice," he remarked.

"I know of your witchcraft, aye," she spat. "Justice Havener used it on us enough times."

"Sir Bronislav Havener, is it?" Vonvalt mused. He knew the man only by name. They had occupied the Grand Lodge—the headquarters of the Magistratum in Sova—concurrently, but briefly, and had never spoken except to exchange professional pleasantries. "You are holding him in the town gaol."

Klement grumbled something which he did not catch.

"Who is he supposed to have murdered?"

"A young boy."

"Is that so?"

"Yes."

"How young?"

"Why does that matter?"

"There is killing a helpless infant, and there is, *exempli gratia*, killing a belligerent lad."

"What difference does it make?"

"Entire cases hinge on these details."

Klement sniffed, and sat back. "About six years old. Just shy of it."

"Where is his body?"

"At sea. Per custom."

"What custom is that?" Vonvalt asked, thinking of the man with the strange accent he had heard on their arrival. Before she could reply, he continued, "this is a strange place. Why is it half empty? And why does no one look Grozodan?"

In so referring to Grozodans—like Bressinger—he was referring to the traditionally dark-haired, olive-skinned natives of the province. But it seemed to him that the majority of the townsfolk in Gdansburg were pale, their hair blonde or red. It was an uncommon lineage on the peninsula.

Klement turned and looked out of the window. She continued to look out of the window as she spoke. "This place was settled by Brigalanders decades ago. Raided, and then settled. They mixed with the locals, put down roots."

"I see," Vonvalt said, nodding. Brigaland lay two hundred nautical miles north of the northernmost part of the contiguous Empire. Every summer, its inhabitants sailed across the Seolhyþa Straits and raided the Imperial coastline, usually at will. Sometimes, as had evidently happened here in Gdansburg, they settled. "Does that explain why the place is half empty?"

"Oh no," Klement said, waving him off. "That happened much more recently. Two years ago, I'd say."

"Oh?"

"It was the lighthouse," she said. "Used to be that Gdansburg was the largest trading port on the Meridian coast. And then one day..." She looked at him briefly. Vonvalt read in her expression anger, but also a second, deeper emotion. She was resentful. Not at his presence, but rather, that he might just have the authority and ability to assist her. "One day..."

"It became infested with something supernatural?"

"Haunted." She gave him another malicious glare, daring him to make fun of her. When he didn't, she said, "you think it risible."

"Few are better acquainted with the arcane than me," Vonvalt said, thinking about the times he had practised necromancy. "But in my experience, the creatures and spirits and other inhabitants of the holy dimensions tend to remain *confined* to the holy dimensions."

"Tend to?"

He gave her a small smile. "Invariably."

She turned away from him again. "I have heard it with my own ears. A dreadful screaming, coming from the lighthouse at night. No one will go near it. No one will light it."

"I see. There were wrecks."

"Two," Klement said, nodding. "That was enough for word to spread. The merchants stopped coming here. They went to Grallstein instead."

"And the town's population followed the coin."

"Leaving us with the dregs. The old, the young, the infirm. We do what we can, here in the abbey. But Gdansburg is a year or two from abandonment. I'm certain of it."

Vonvalt felt some sympathy for the woman then, in spite of her prickliness.

"I was told the sheriff is dead."

"Aye. He died around the same time actually."

"Oh?"

"It is not what you think. He was old. Unwell."

"It is not his spirit which lingers in the lighthouse?"

She shook her head. "The screaming is that of a woman."

"I see." He paused. "You will tell me nothing further about Justice Havener?"

"Why? Are you going to drag it out of me with sorcery?"

"If I must."

"Do as you please."

He sighed. He did briefly think about using the Voice on her again, but he decided that it would be better to try and make an ally of her—if he could.

"Very well," he said eventually. "We shall speak again soon."

She snorted, but did not reply.

Vonvalt nodded to himself, and left.

✦

BRESSINGER WAS TALKING to a pretty young nun outside the abbey's main door when Vonvalt swept past him.

"Come on, Dubine," he said, and his taskman fell into step beside him.

"Well? Where are they holding him?"

"The town gaol."

"I daresay we could have deduced that without an interrogation."

"I daresay you are right."

"Who is it?"

"Bronislav Havener."

Bressinger shook his head. "I don't know him."

"There's not much to know."

They made their way back into the town, though not far; the gaol was located on a sizeable distributary from the main thoroughfare. Vonvalt found that the placement of town gaols and stockades tended to depend on whether they also contained the sheriff's office. If they did, they were situated on relatively pleasant streets. If they did not, they were lumped in with the town's unsociable trades closure—the butchers, tanneries, and so on.

Here the former seemed to be the case, for the road was cobbled and quite agreeable, lined with cypress trees and planters filled with indigenous wildflowers. Indeed, a little further on, Vonvalt spotted a blue star, the Imperial mark of a licensed physician.

"There you are, Dubine; he could have your… issue examined."

"I'd rather be having my issue examined by that nun," he growled, and Vonvalt chuckled despite himself.

The smile quickly faded from his lips as they drew level with the gaol door. Attached to it was a note, which read:

Witch inside!
He has the power to compel you against your will!
For your own safety, do not enter!

Next to it was a crude diagram for the illiterate, which in other circumstances would have been amusing.

"Bloody hell," Bressinger said. "They really do have him in there."

"Apparently," Vonvalt replied, turning the handle. "Come on."

Inside it was dingy. The cheap tallow candles had all long ago burnt out, and there was a strong smell of urine. Vonvalt reached into his pocket and pulled out a small kerchief filled with lavender, harvested locally, and held it to his nose.

"Who's there?" a powerful voice demanded.

"Justice Sir Konrad Vonvalt."

"Oh thank Nema. Thank the gods and all the saints."

"Don't thank them just yet," Bressinger said quietly.

They drew level with the far cell. Another notice was posted there, this one reading:

Cover your ears!

"Justice Sir Bronislav Havener," Vonvalt said, peering through the barred square hole cut into the door.

"Konrad, by Nema it is good to see you."

Vonvalt appraised the man. He looked to be in good health, though there was no evidence of victuals having been provided. He was about fifteen years older than Vonvalt, putting him in his mid-forties. He had thinning, greying hair, was bearded, and was not overweight so much as bullish, possessed of a naturally large, muscular frame.

"Get me some ale, would you? I'm about to expire."

Bressinger turned and headed to the nearest public house. Once the main door was closed, Vonvalt turned back to Havener.

"What's going on? Why have these people detained you?"

"Certainly on no legal authority. Release me, Sir Konrad, and I shall be on my way."

Vonvalt paused. "I will release you, in due course," he replied carefully. "But I should like to hear what has happened before I do."

"You bloody idiot, fetch the keys immediately! I'll not explain myself!"

"As you wish," Vonvalt said, and immediately turned on his heel.

"For Nema's—wait, damn you. Are you fetching the keys, or are you leaving?"

"I'm leaving."

"Just—bloody—just *wait* there a moment. Come back here, for the gods' *sakes.*" Vonvalt returned. "You always had a reputation for being such a stickler."

"My reputation, I hope, is one of prudence."

"Your reputation, *Justice*, is for being the Emperor's favoured whelp."

Vonvalt accepted this, as he had to. To deny it would have been to deny the objective truth. "I have had His Excellency's ear these past few years," he said. "I'll make no bones about it."

"A Jägelander, too. A man whose father took the Highmark. Not even a trueborn Sovan."

"I fought and bled in the Legions. I have done more than most for the Empire," Vonvalt growled, bristling. There was nothing in the world that got under his skin more than pompous old Sovans reminding him of his heritage. As though it were a failing.

As though it were a weakness.

"I take my leave," he said, before he lost his temper.

"Wait!" Havener blurted out. "I am sorry. Sir Konrad, wait, please. I *am* sorry. Look at me." He gestured to the urine-soaked floor of his cell. "Look at where they are keeping me."

"Why are they keeping you at all?"

Havener looked at him sidelong. "What have they told you?"

"That you killed a boy. A young one."

"Killed a boy," Havener muttered bitterly. "Preposterous."

"Whether or not it is preposterous, they certainly believe you to have done it. Believe it most assuredly."

"Oh assuredly? *Assuredly*! A bunch of bloody Brigalander mongrels, accusing *me* of murder! *Infanticide*?! I mean really, Sir Konrad, *really*!"

"I take it that you deny the charge."

"Oh for Nema's sake. You are not indulging this nonsense, are you? You are not actually entertaining that I might have done it?"

Vonvalt shook his head. "Sir Bronislav, I find it very difficult to believe that a Justice is capable of murder, given the rigours of our training and our ethics."

Havener nodded. "Precisely. Precisely!"

"But you of all people will know that that same training and code of ethics binds me very strictly to the proper investigative procedures."

It took Havener three heartbeats to realise what Vonvalt was saying. When he did, he sighed angrily, and rolled his eyes. "Terrific. I'm going to be investigated like a base criminal."

"The common law demands nothing less."

"I would expect *nothing less* from you," Havener sneered. "I said, did I not: your reputation is that of a stickler."

Vonvalt took this in his stride. "Do you know what your reputation is, Sir Bronislav?"

He glowered. "No."

"Neither do I," Vonvalt replied, and left.

II
THE LIGHTHOUSE

"It is of vital importance to the health and integrity of any judicial apparatus that its executive arm—sheriffs, lawkeepers, magistrates, and wardens—are held not to the same standard as the commonfolk, but to a higher one. An officer of the Crown enjoys a position of special authority over his countrymen, and special authority must always attract burdensome obligations."

—From Caterhauser's *The Sovan Criminal Code: Advice to Practitioners*

"BLOODY ARSEHOLE," VONVALT muttered as Bressinger exited the physician's.

"I'm sure the doctor has a lotion for that," Bressinger replied, but when Vonvalt did not laugh, his own good mood evaporated. "What's the matter?"

"Even if he's innocent, I'd be tempted to let him rot."

"But that would be false imprisonment!" Bressinger replied in a stentorian voice.

"I'm not in the mood, Dubine."

"Got under your skin, did he?"

"Like a tick."

The two men walked down the street, drawing looks from every passerby.

"What did he say?"

"Just a bare denial. I'll speak to him again tomorrow when my blood is cooled."

"What will you do now? Want me to find us some lodgings?"

"Please. I'm going to go and have a look at this lighthouse."

"Really? The haunted one?"

"It's not haunted," Vonvalt snapped. He looked ahead to the town's main thoroughfare. He pointed. "There, The Brass Wyvern," he said, spying a public house. "I'll meet you in the common room in about an hour."

VONVALT PICKED HIS way across the town and then up to the headland—a scrubby, rocky protuberance of silt- and sandstone that jutted out into the Meridian Ocean for several hundred feet. To the north, an abandoned harbour protected several acres of brine from the vicissitudes of the wind—the same wind which battered him as he approached the old fortress. Here the smell of the saltmarsh to the south was strong. It was vast, its underpinning soil peat-dark, and was well stocked with birds and insects.

The outermost gate was rotted through and open, and he entered a small, overgrown courtyard. Here was a measure of respite, a surprisingly quiet space where the walls protected the enclosure from the wind. He looked up at the keep, and the tower beyond it, an ornate, crenellated structure that was more manor house than fortress. All of it was crumbling under the iron grip of rampant pyracantha, whose bright orange berries littered the ground, curiously untouched by the local birds.

In spite of his easy, arrogant dismissal of the townsfolk's fears, he felt a creeping sense of unease in that gloomy, isolated place. But then the sun appeared beneath the low ceiling of cloud, and Vonvalt, comforted in the same way a frightened child might be, entered the keep.

It was unremarkable. A small disarming chamber, followed by an entrance hall hanging with mildewed tapestries. Here was a strong smell of mould, as well as evidence of unlawful occupation: soot from cookfires staining the floor, desiccated human waste, discarded scraps of food—

Vonvalt paused, brow furrowed. Much like the berries in the courtyard, food scraps should certainly have been carried off by vermin.

"Hm," he grunted. He stood in the entrance hall for a long time, head cocked, listening. But there was nothing except the rhythmic pounding of the waves, the wash of the retreating tide, and the odd distant shout, dog bark, and metallic clang from the town.

Eventually he made his way through to the lighthouse tower and ascended. Here the wind moaned through embrasures, a haunting sound which initially set his heart thumping, before he chuckled at his own silliness. Still, just before he reached the top, and the trapdoor there, he called out, "If there is anybody in there, make yourself known now. I am an Imperial Justice, and I am armed."

Silence.

"Hellfire," he muttered, drawing his short sword. Then, with a sudden burst of speed, he charged the lantern room.

It was empty.

He sighed, and slid his sword back into its scabbard. Then, after doing a turn around the unlit brazier, he pushed open the door to the gallery which encircled the lantern room, and stepped outside.

"Nema," he swore as he was battered by gale-force winds roaring off the ocean. The Meridian was choppy from wind-over-tide, and whitecaps frothed and churned as far as the eye could see.

Standing there on the edge of the Empire instilled within him a vertiginous feeling of isolation, a reminder of his incredible insignificance in the world. Somewhere across that many thousands of miles of ocean were the I'Kamataxians, a strange, foreign people whom the fruits of scholarship and trade obliged Vonvalt to believe existed, though he had never seen them. Every year hundreds of Sovan sailors attempted to make the crossing in their huge merchant carracks, but only a small handful returned. Still, the incredible riches they returned with—holdsful of jadestone, obsidian, copper, and gold; exotic pelts and feathers; and a type of bitter brown bean which Vonvalt was assured was very popular as a drink in the lands of the wolfmen—were proof enough that there was something beyond the great blue borders of the known world.

Vonvalt's heart leapt as a scream ripped through the lighthouse.

"Gods' blood!" he cried out, snatching hold of the merlon in front of him. He turned, expecting some spectral figure to be advancing on him through the lantern room, but it remained empty.

He stood, straining to hear, trying to convince himself that it was just a person suffering some injury in Gdansburg. But there had been a closeness and clarity to the scream which left its provenance beyond doubt.

The lighthouse itself.

"Nema," he muttered, his heart still palpitating wildly. Suddenly he didn't want to re-enter the lighthouse; but behind him, the sun was setting, and he *certainly* didn't want to be inside it after dark.

In that moment, a second scream cut through the air, but this time it was not something arcane and discorporate; instead it came from a large marsh harrier circling the tower. It was a magnificent bird, its feathers a rich golden brown, its wingtips black. It performed several passes of Vonvalt, before perching on the merlon next to him.

He looked at the harrier. It looked back, examining him with an intelligence that went well beyond the avian.

"Resi," Vonvalt said with relief. The bird cawed a few times, bobbing its head and ruffling its feathers. "I didn't realise you were this close."

The bird cawed again, and then launched itself off the lighthouse and soared out across the coast. Vonvalt smiled and shook his head, his fear forgotten.

It didn't stop him exiting the fortress at a run, though.

✦

"I SAID A public house, not a brothel," Vonvalt said, looking about the common room.

"I believe what you *actually* said," Bressinger replied, examining the buttocks of a passing prostitute with relish, "was to meet you in the common room of the Brass Wyvern in an hour."

Vonvalt sighed. "You should not be getting your end away in your condition. You will pass on the pox."

"Keep your—I would never do that," Bressinger hissed; then he clacked his tongue and performed a masturbatory gesture with his hand. "I can still get a—"

"By Nema, Dubine, how have you not learnt by now that I'm not interested in your proclivities."

"I learnt it long ago. I just enjoy annoying you."

"Never a truer word was spoken," Vonvalt said, and approached the bar.

"What'll it be, my lord Justice?" the man asked with a mixture of nerves and anger.

"Word spreads."

"Aye. That it does. I hope you've not come to take your friend away."

"He's no friend of mine. And do not threaten me. It is a crime."

The barkeep straightened up, stony faced. "What'll it be?"

"Do you have any wine?"

"Hm. Somewhere in the back."

"What about food?"

"There's some hog leftover from yesterday. Cold cuts only."

"What about lodgings?"

"Aye."

"Without interruptions," he said, gesturing to the prostitutes.

"You'll still have to pay. Girls've got to eat too."

"That's fine," Vonvalt said, thumbing down several marks on to the counter—an extraordinary sum. The barkeep managed to keep his composure, although Vonvalt saw the glint of hunger in his eyes.

"Can't take marks here."

"Of course you can. This is perfectly legal tender."

"Maybe in Annholt, but not this far west. Do you have any florins?"

"Not that I'm willing to part with," Vonvalt grumbled, though he produced a purse full of them. "What's the going rate?"

The man licked his lips. "Hundred to one."

"Fuck off!" Vonvalt scoffed out, drawing the attention of all the patrons and prostitutes in the common room. "I will give you fifty; otherwise I can give you zero and a charge for extortion."

"As you will, my lord," the barkeep said, humiliated, and accepted the money.

"See that we are not disturbed."

"As you will."

Vonvalt returned to Bressinger, and sat down.

"How was the lighthouse?" Bressinger asked.

"You know, Dubine," Vonvalt sighed. "I think there might be something to it."

"You're joking."

Vonvalt shook his head. "Got a very strange feeling in that place. And I certainly heard a scream."

"Probably the local blacksmith breaking his thumb."

"No. No... it was very strange. Very eerie. By the way, Resi August is on her way."

Bressinger brightened. "Justice Lady August," he said, and then shoved Vonvalt. "No wonder you don't want to be caught in a brothel."

"I don't want to be caught in a brothel at all."

"Why do you pretend to be above such things? I know you partake."

"I'm not talking about this."

"We can talk about my urethra again?"

A serving girl appeared, carrying two trenchers containing roast hog, carrot, turnip, and potato, all covered in piping hot gravy. She bustled off, and a moment later returned with a bottle of wine and a pewter goblet.

"Thank you," Vonvalt said, handing her a groat.

"What's next, then?" Bressinger asked.

"Well, tomorrow I must hold court," Vonvalt replied, tucking in to his dinner. "But after that, I shall have to find out more about this alleged murder. See what you can dig up. They say the body is out to sea, per an old Brigalander custom. But loosen some tongues."

"Aye, will do." Bressinger replied through his mouthful.

AN HOUR LATER, Vonvalt was in bed and about to extinguish his candle when there was a knock at his door.

"I said I was not to be disturbed."

The door opened notwithstanding. Vonvalt was about to issue an angry reprimand—he was more annoyed with himself that he had forgotten to lock it—when he saw Justice August standing in the doorway.

"Resi," he said, his heart surging. "You are earlier than I expected."

She smiled at him. She was a beautiful woman, of an age with Vonvalt, with raven dark hair that came past her shoulders and fine, unmarked skin. He stood, and moved to meet her. "That was you, by the lighthouse?"

She nodded. "Yes. We need to talk about that. There is something—" "Later, later," he said, and moved in to kiss her.

"Konrad! Let me at least have a wash first," she said, gesturing to the bowl of water in the corner of the room.

"No," he protested. "I want you as you are."

"Nema, you are disgusting," she said, slapping him on the chest. "You are as bad as Dubine, though you affect not to be."

"I am nothing like Dubine. That man is an animal."

"All men are animals, highborn and low. Equally feral. Equally disgusting."

He gripped her elbows. "I *need* you."

"And you are very welcome to me!" she laughed. "*After* I have washed."

A LITTLE WHILE later, they lay on the mattress, naked and postcoital and sheened with sweat.

"Konrad Vonvalt," Resi said, chewing on a wad of silphium leaves. "Unstoppable in the courtroom, stoppable in the bedroom."

Vonvalt snorted, wiping the sweat from his forehead. "It's been a while, Resi. Give me a moment to gather myself."

"That's what they all say," she said, and though her tone was wry and playful, Vonvalt's humour evaporated.

"You have been seeing other men?"

"Oh, I've been seeing all sorts," she replied. She turned briefly to him, catching his expression. "Let's not do this again, Konrad. You know you and I can never form a partnership. I see you but once every half-year, and that is on the very best case."

Vonvalt hated hearing these home truths. "I ache for you. Every part of me."

"Absence makes the heart grow fonder."

"Resi, please."

"You know you will always be special to me. Forever. But I cannot commit myself to you, and the reasons why are very well-rehearsed."

"I know," he sighed. "I am sorry for bringing it up again."

"Oh, do not apologise. I grapple with it as you do."

They lay in comfortable silence, each of them replaying the countless decisions they had made over the course of their lives which had led them to this place, both quietly lamenting the mutual exclusivity of being an Imperial Magistrate and marriage.

"They shall think you a whore," he mused out loud. "The other patrons."

Resi shrugged. "Let them think it. I shall not deny myself one of life's greatest pleasures simply because Sova frowns upon 'overindulgence' as improper."

"I am in full agreement with you."

"No, you are not," she said, though the mood was not sour. "You have contrived to become ever more Imperial since the day we met. You are so desperate for them to welcome you as one of their own. You adopt their mores as though you had been born to them."

"Don't you start. Now you sound like Havener."

"I've heard about this. What's going on with him?"

"The townsfolk claim he murdered a small boy. I've yet to get to the nub of it. That's a job for tomorrow."

"Well. I shall help you, if you wish."

"Absolutely."

"And with the matter of the lighthouse."

"Tomorrow, please," he said, unwilling to be burdened with it now.

They lay in silence once again.

"What's it like?" he asked eventually, tracing a line around her left nipple. "Wearing a bird like that? Its mind like a glove."

Resi shrugged. "Curiously unexhilarating. The bird thinks nothing of flight, and so neither do I, in the moment."

Vonvalt smiled. "What happens if you are approached by a bird suitor?"

"Are you asking me how birds fuck? Nema, you deviant. What do you want me to do, lay an egg for you?"

He laughed, and she laughed, and they turned their bodies towards each other for another round.

III
THE BUSINESS OF JUSTICE

"It is impossible for the lawkeeper to prevent every crime. Civilised society recognises this. To prevent every crime would require the full engagement of the state's entire apparatus, and even then it would not be enough. What then, to do? The lawkeeper need only prevent, solve, or prosecute a sample of crimes. How large a sample? Enough that the commonfolk fear the consequences of being caught more than they covet the rewards of commission."

—From Caterhauser's *The Sovan Criminal Code: Advice to Practitioners*

HE SET UP court the next day, liberating the Duke of Brondsey's cart of all its accoutrements. These consisted of a large table and chair; a pole upon which was a shield bearing the device of House Haugenate—the Imperial household; ledgers; bottles of ink and quills; and other texts and legal paraphernalia. They put it all in the central square, which was joined north and south by the town's high street, drawing a great deal of attention as they did so.

"You should take on an apprentice to help you with this shit,"

Bressinger said, affecting to grunt as he dumped the heavy tomes of legal precedent on the desk next to Vonvalt.

"Perhaps I shall, one day."

"Who would you have? They would foist some noble scion on you."

"It is not their business to foist anyone on me. Besides," he said, musing for a moment. "I would much rather elevate some gutter waif."

"What good will milk from the Great Wolf's teat do for an uneducated vagrant?"

"Must be the liberal urban sensibilities I am so often accused of harbouring," Vonvalt replied. "Peace, now; here comes a complainant."

They spent the morning dealing with the legal complaints of the townsfolk. Some had already been dealt with by the de facto legal authority of Matria Klement, apparently unsatisfactorily. But Vonvalt was surprised to find that she was a fine administrator of justice, and was surprised further by how much he agreed with her pronouncements.

"This is a waste of time," Bressinger muttered when he returned with their lunch. In his hand he held an onion, which he had taken a large bite out of. "Three hours of this shite and nothing more interesting than affray."

"You realise that is a good thing, don't you?"

"Give us something juicy. Something to really get our teeth into."

"Dubine, we are investigating a charge of murder against a fellow Justice."

"Are we?" Bressinger asked sharply. "Because it seems to me you are doing everything in your power to avoid it."

"What rot!" Vonvalt snapped, furious at being put on the back foot.

"Justices can commit crimes too, Konrad."

"*Sir* Konrad."

"Oh, you are going to be like that, are you?"

Vonvalt waved him off. "You are being ferociously irritating this morning."

"'Tis past noon. The man has been accused of murder, and you are sitting here dealing with this nonsense."

Vonvalt took a few deep breaths. "I *know* Justices are capable of committing crimes—"

"Do you?"

"—*but*! They are honourable men and women. It is profoundly unlikely."

Bressinger shrugged. "Why? He is a man like any other."

"'Like any other'? Please. The strictures by which we live our lives—"

"Oh, spare me. I'm not one of your students."

"Fine. You want to grapple with this matter now?"

"Absolutely I do."

"Fetch me the boy's family then. They have not come to make a complaint to me here. I have not heard a charge of murder levelled against him except in the most spurious and vague of circumstances. Fetch them to me, and I shall deal with the matter here and now."

"Nema," Bressinger muttered, tossing the onion away. "You are normally happier after a tumble with Resi."

"Be about it!" Vonvalt thundered, to the shock of those townsfolk waiting to petition.

"As you wish, your worshipfulness," Bressinger replied, and sauntered off.

✦

HE RETURNED A little while later, this time with Matria Klement in tow.

"That is not who I asked for," Vonvalt said, looking up briefly from where he was writing the final judgment in his ledger—an unwanted hair cutting, which engendered a fine for civil battery.

"And yet, it is who you have," Klement snapped. "If you think you can waltz up here, and demand an audience with a grieving family—"

"I am not *demanding* an *audience*," Vonvalt thundered. "I am requesting a *witness* give *evidence* to support an *allegation*." He levelled a finger at her. "An extremely serious allegation. And if you think you and your fellows here can imprison an Imperial Justice without trial, and do Nema-knows-what to him, you are all in for a *rude* awakening. Like it or not, Matria, Grozoda is a Sovan possession, subject to Sovan laws and procedures. My authority here knows no bounds save the limits the Emperor Himself sees fit to set. If there is a complaint of murder to be made—the most serious crime it is possible to commit short of treason!—*fetch* the complainants to me this *instant*, or I shall turn Justice Havener loose and be on my way!"

"Fucking hell," Klement grumbled, looking as though she might fall over. Around her, shopfronts and residents' windows were lousy with onlookers. Even Bressinger, who was as familiar with Vonvalt as it was possible to be, looked utterly aghast at the outburst.

Klement approached the table. Now she appeared to be frightened. "Will you come with me?" she asked quietly. "Please. The boy is two days dead. Please do not interrogate them here, in public, for all to see."

Vonvalt was trembling with self-righteous anger, and took several deep breaths to calm himself. He even considered apologising, but decided against it.

"Fine," he said. "Dubine, where is Resi?"

"I don't—"

"Fetch her, would you?" He gestured to the street ahead. "All right, Matria. Lead on."

THE PARENTS WERE in precisely the state Vonvalt had anticipated: pale, washed out, red-eyed, and inconsolable. They lived in a modest house in what would have been, in a typical Sovan settlement, the northern closure of the town. Here it was mostly residences, basic structures of adobe with thatched roofs, though some were entirely made of dry stone, whilst other roofs were laid with sod rather than thatch. The most striking thing was an old Brigalander longboat, which had been pulled ashore, upended, and repurposed as the roof to a community centre.

Vonvalt was gestured inside, where he was greeted by a surprisingly large hall with space for a dozen permanent residents. The whole house was open—that was to say, there were no internal walls—with different areas set aside for sleeping, cooking, and recreation.

He was a Reichskrieg veteran, and had investigated, prosecuted, and executed dozens of criminals in the course of his career—including enemies of the state in enormous set piece trials in the Royal Imperial Courts of Justice in Sova. But here, faced with the furious grief of bereaved parents, he withered.

"I..." he began, suddenly finding himself at a loss for words. The sorrow filled the house like a cloud, suffocating him.

"You're one of them," the mother snarled. Like the father, she was blonde haired and pale skinned, and looked emaciated with grief. "*Autunska. Autunska*!"

It was a common Northerner epithet, and meant 'wolf shit'.

"I'm here to help," Vonvalt said, clearing his throat several times until he found his voice. "I am here to help you. I've come to speak to you about what happened."

He looked over as Klement spoke quickly and quietly in an unfamiliar pagan tongue. Whatever it was, it seemed to harden the mother against him—not that she needed much in the way of hardening.

"What are your names?" Vonvalt asked gently. When it looked as though Klement was about to cut in again, he said to her sharply, "interrupt once more and I shall have you arrested."

The mother sniffled. "Freya," she muttered.

"And I am Erik," the father said.

"I am Sir Konrad Vonvalt. I am an Imperial Magistrate."

"You are the same as him," Freya said, tears rolling down her cheeks.

"I can assure you, madam, I am not."

"What do you want?" Erik asked.

"I want to find out what happened."

"He wants to release Havener," Klement said.

Vonvalt rounded on her. "Right," he said, at the same moment that Bressinger and August entered. "Dubine; take Matria Klement away and put her in the gaol."

Bressinger's eyes widened. "Sire?"

"Immediately, please."

"Don't touch me," Klement snarled. She said something else quickly to the grieving parents, before following Bressinger out.

"Who's she?" one of the longhouse's other occupants nodded to August.

"She's a colleague," Vonvalt said, struggling to remain calm. Nema, but that bloody matria got under his skin. Why couldn't they see he was trying to help?

This prompted another bout of chatter in that same Northerner language. The parents seemed to fold in on themselves. The others became agitated.

"What have you done?" August asked him quietly, taking him to one side.

Vonvalt pinched the bridge of his nose. "Handled this rather badly, I fear."

"They don't trust you."

"Yes. I had reached that conclusion."

"Can you blame them?"

"No. But that does not make it less frustrating. I have told them I am here to help."

"Aye. Havener probably said the same thing."

Vonvalt glanced over to the parents, who were now being enveloped by their friends and family members in a large group embrace.

"I have great sympathy for these people—"

"You are doing an excellent job of concealing it."

Vonvalt sighed. "What would you have me do, Resi? These people are obligated to assist me."

August looked at him wide-eyed. "What is the *matter* with you?" she hissed.

Vonvalt shook his head. "Nothing. This business with the lighthouse is troubling me," he said. It was only partly a lie.

"I need to discuss that with you. Here; you are going to do naught but damage, now. I have an idea."

Vonvalt cast one final look at the bereaved family. "Fine."

✦

A LITTLE WHILE later they were in a private room in the Brass Wyvern, a place normally reserved for young naked women to gyrate seductively whilst being ogled. Here the seniormost Imperial lawkeepers west of Annholt gathered to lay plans.

"It is clear that Havener has destroyed any trust in the Imperial justice system in Gdansburg," August said once their food and drink had been brought in, and the door closed and bolted.

"Verily," Vonvalt muttered.

"So the more you flounce about demanding respect and obeisance from everyone, the more you are going to harden their resolve to ignore you." Vonvalt opened his mouth to angrily respond, but was silenced when August held up a hand. "I am not finished."

Next to them, Bressinger chuckled.

"The damage has already been done. So; we must be more subtle in our investigations."

Vonvalt reclined, and nodded. "All right. What is it you suggest?"

"Release Klement this evening."

"Preposterous. I mean to bring her up on a charge, not let her go."

August rolled her eyes. "Konrad, be serious a moment! Look at this place. It is dying. There is no trade. There is barely any farmland. All of the young and able-bodied have left. Klement, like her or not—"

"I most assuredly do not."

"—is the linchpin holding it together. By publicly butting heads with her, all you are doing is turning everyone against you. And then you will have no choice but to release Havener, because no one will give you any evidence."

"But that is precisely the problem. All of them seem to be labouring under the misapprehension that they can simply wait out my time here. That if they just hold out long enough, I will go, and leave Havener to be lynched."

"That is undoubtedly the case," August said. "So we must ensure that justice is done before our departure."

"Tell me of your plan."

"Release Klement. She will go back to the parents, I'm certain of it. And they are certain to discuss details of the matter—sensitive details."

"You mean to have Dubine eavesdrop on them?"

She shook her head. "No. Me. I shall take the form of some small creature; a mouse or rat or wren. Then I shall tell you what I hear."

Vonvalt considered this. "Yes," he said. "Yes, that sounds like a good plan."

"You could also just speak to Havener again?" Bressinger said. "Haven't given that sack of shit a proper questioning, yet."

"I will. But I don't want to speak to him until I have some more information. I don't want him to colour my thoughts."

The three of them sat in silence.

"Do you need any special preparation?"

August shook her head. "No. But I must be somewhere private during the ritual. When I should be grateful if you would… not *guard* me, per se, but—"

"I understand. We can do it in my bedchamber."

Bressinger raised an eyebrow.

"Finish your dinner," Vonvalt muttered to him, as August took a turn chuckling. "Then you can go and let Klement free."

"As you will."

"You had better take Havener some more victuals as well. Seems he will be detained a little while longer."

IV
OF MICE AND MEN

"To what lengths may a lawkeeper go in enforcing the law? May he or she break it? The answer is, of course, no, but evidence obtained through illegal means is not automatically inadmissible. The Justice, or warden, must weigh the probative value of the evidence as against the malfeasance of the lawkeeper, the nature of the defendant's alleged crimes, and the need for robust due process. Compelling evidence of innocence or guilt should be considered even in the face of spectacular wrongdoing, if it serves the cause of justice."

—From Caterhauser's *The Sovan Criminal Code: Advice to Practitioners*

SHE CHOSE A dormouse in the end. It was not without risk; their brains and minds were small, and could be easily overwhelmed by the psychic loading of a human. But they had excellent night vision and hearing, they were discreet and quick, and they were everywhere. No one would bat an eyelid seeing a mouse in the beams.

She lay down on Vonvalt's mattress and closed her eyes, breathing her way into a deep trance. Then she extended her consciousness out, questing, until she found what she was looking for. There were thousands of them, these mice, pinpricks of fuzzy light in a roiling sea of grey aether. These moments always amused her, as she saw just how many of these creatures people considered vermin were in and amongst them—wild pigs and dogs, wolves, foxes, rats, and mice. All had learnt to avoid humans, but they were there, and they were legion.

There followed an uncomfortable period in which she tethered herself to the little creature. She selected a young, healthy one, and for a few moments was literally in two minds. She felt her coccyx sprout a tail; felt the curious sensation of her arms as they felt more like a second pair of legs; found the nature of the dormouse mixing with her own, sharing its impulses and prey-fears.

Larger animals resisted this process. As an initiate in the Magistratum, learning how to control this power, it had been possible for creatures to throw her out of their brains entirely. But the dormouse was small and had little in the way of mental faculty, and she was able to crush its natural impulse to resist with ease.

"Are you all right?" Vonvalt asked her, a most unwelcome and irritating interruption, for she had specifically told him not to say anything. She waved him off in what would be her last conscious act as a human for a little while. Then she fully let go of her human self. They had warned her, years before, that every time she used the power, she would lose a tiny part of her. A little sliver of her mind, an iota; not enough to do anything by itself, but that was the problem with small things. A lot of them together turned into big things.

She scurried through the town, and watched Dubine release Klement, who seemed extremely displeased; then she followed the matria through the streets of Gdansburg. For a dismal moment, she feared that Klement was heading straight back to the abbey, and that all of her clever conjecture was just that. Indeed, Klement initially walked straight past the street on which the parents lived, and continued on, and then spent some time in conversation with sundry townsfolk. August was about to release her grip on the dormouse, for there was no sense in degrading her psychic powers for no reason, but then Klement did turn towards Freya and Erik's longhouse, and she scuttled after, a tiny trespasser.

She watched as Klement was welcomed into the house, and embraced tightly, and then quickly climbed up the outer wall and found a gap in the thatch of the roof. She was easily able to slip through on to one of the load-bearing beams, and there she perched, and observed.

And groaned—which, amusingly, came out as a muffled squeak—as they began speaking in the native tongue of Brigalanders.

It had been an unforgivable oversight, the kind of minor detail that she as a Justice should have been alive to. She was once again about to release her grip on the dormouse, when after several minutes, Klement said, "I'm sorry. It has been a long and tiring day, and I must speak Saxan."

"Of course," Freya said. "Of course. Come, sit. You must be exhausted."

They sat. There were only the parents and Klement present now, any other children and family members absent.

"What do they want?" Freya asked.

"To release their fellow," Klement said harshly. The man, Erik, looked unimpressed by this.

"So you say," he said, eyes red-rimmed. "But *they* said they were investigating the matter."

"Well of course they are going to say that, aren't they?" Klement replied, though she did seem to be genuinely exhausted—unsurprising, since she was an old woman—and did not have the energy to sustain her anger.

"If they were going to release him, would they not have just done it? They are a law unto themselves. The only way we could stop them is by fighting them," Freya said.

"I have heard of the man. Sir Konrad. He is supposed be one of the finest swordsmen Sova has ever produced," Erik murmured.

"We aren't going to fight them. We stick to the original plan. We just tell them nothing and wait until they leave."

"And if they try and release Havener?"

"Then we kill him."

Erik shook his head again. "I don't like this. Why don't we just speak with them? We are just going to get ourselves into more trouble."

"White Nema, your blood is water!" Klement snapped.

"Peace, Matria, peace," Freya said, wiping her eyes. "I just don't *understand* it. He was a normal boy, a happy boy. And then he suffered that mental malaise after the first time."

"After the first time?" August thought, and somewhere in the distance, heard her human self murmuring these words out loud.

"Was as though his mind just… went," Erik said, nodding. "Like steam off tea."

"And then that screaming," Freya continued in a haunted tone. "White Nema, he was so afraid. So terrified of that Justice. Why was he screaming *so much*?"

"Hush, child hush," Klement soothed, reaching out her hands and taking hold of the mother's. "You are going to upset yourself, reliving it."

"I can do naught else!" she suddenly wailed. "*Why* did he *die*?"

"The Justice did it," Klement said forcefully. "Everyone saw it."

"But we *didn't*," Erik said. "That's just it, Radmila. We didn't *see* anything. You keep saying it was Havener, but he didn't actually do anything."

"Whose side are you on?" the matria demanded.

"I'm on the side of my boy!" Erik thundered, and then, after a few tense moments, calmed himself. "But I want to understand what happened. Osgar wasn't stabbed. He wasn't hit about the head. Havener didn't lay a finger on him. If you had looked at Osgar when we put him out to sea, you would have thought he was merely sleeping. And yet everyone says the Justice murdered him."

"Because he did! He had to have done."

"But how? Why?"

"To stop his screaming. You remember the screaming. Freya certainly does."

"Of course I remember it. But the boy had lost his wits. All sorts would upset him since the first time."

"The first time, the first time for what*?"* August urged.

"Not like that," Klement said, shaking her head. "This was something else. And he used his magick to silence him. I'm certain of it. I'm *certain* of it, Freya, and I will not let these Imperials come here to protect one of their own. That's all they're here for. That's all they're good for."

"For goodness' sake, Radmila!" Erik snapped. "If they were here to release him, he would have been released!"

Klement jabbed a thumb into her breastbone. "I *loved* that boy. You know how much I looked after him, how much we helped with him in the abbey. For two years the nuns tended him—"

"We know," Freya said, defeated. "We know. And we are grateful for everything."

Klement sighed. "No," she said, shaking her head. "No. *I* am sorry. I cannot begin to imagine the feeling. And here I've come barging in, shouting at you, lecturing you—"

"No, no," Erik said, but August was no longer paying attention. Her little dormouse heart surged violently. Her ears twitched, her blood—such a minuscule quantity of it!—pulsed like liquid rock.

There was a tabby cat, and it had moved so quickly and quietly across the beam that she had not seen it. With a vertiginous sense of prey-fear, she turned and fled, hearing the cat's claws scratching and scrabbling against the wooden beam behind her with all the cacophonous thunder of trees being uprooted in a storm. August had been in the mind of the mouse for just long enough to forget that she could untether herself at will, and the part of her human mind normally present as a failsafe was being overridden and ignored by the sheer terror of the chase.

She squeaked and scrabbled down the side of the wall, pursued with relentless speed and feline ferocity. The cat was faster than her, and was gaining ground quickly.

"Resi? Resi? What's happening?"

The voice, ghostly and familiar, rose up out of the aether.

"Resi?"

Konrad.

She turned. The cat pounced, claws out, teeth bared—

✦

VONVALT STOOD OVER her, gripping her by the shoulders.

"What the hell happened?" he demanded.

"I'm all right," she said. He watched as she examined herself with her hands, feeling for a tail that was not there. "I'm all right. I'm not hurt."

"What happened? You were moaning and thrashing and all sorts."

She sat up, wiping the sweat from her eyes. "Bloody *cat*," she said. He looked down at her, and his expression turned from one of fear and concern, to one of cautious amusement. To his relief, she snorted, and so he chuckled, and then they both shared a brief laugh.

"You need to be more careful," he said, his expression serious.

"I know that."

"Did you learn anything?"

"The boy was suffering from some sort of mental malady," she said. "He had been in the care of the abbey for a couple of years."

"What sort of malady? As in, he'd lost his wits?"

"Yes, but I got the sense that it hadn't always been the case. They kept referring to a 'first time'. As in, the boy had been functioning normally until this 'first time', which apparently was about two years ago. Then he lost his critical faculties and had to be constantly cared for. And then, coinciding with the arrival of Justice Havener, the boy was killed—or died."

"Did they say anything about the slaying?"

"The father seemed to harbour doubts."

"Oh?"

"It is a curious thing; it seems like the boy started screaming when he laid eyes on Havener, and then… just died."

"He was not struck?"

"Apparently not. Not according to the father. In fact, the boy was visibly unharmed."

"So his heart stopped."

August shrugged. "Possibly. Without a physician, we will never know."

"They put the boy out to sea, according to their custom. If he were here, I would have him exhumed."

"And earn yourself a lynching in the process."

"I daresay you are right," Vonvalt muttered darkly. "By Nema, what a strange case." He thought for a moment. "Do you know something interesting?"

"What?"

"When Dubine and I arrived yesterday, and we spoke to Matria Klement, she said the sheriff died around two years ago."

August considered this. "Did she have anything else to say on the matter?"

"That his death was not suspicious."

"Insofar as she was concerned."

"Well, quite."

"I wonder if he kept records?"

"He would have been obliged to, per Sovan ordinances."

"What Sova dictates, and what actually happens—"

"Yes, yes, spare me," Vonvalt said. "I shall turn Dubine to the task. I must say I find that a rather extraordinary coincidence."

Vonvalt began to pace the room, thinking. Then he stopped. "You said you wanted to speak to me about the lighthouse?"

"Oh yes. Just that I have a feeling about it."

Vonvalt waited for her to continue, and when she did not, said, "a feeling?"

"When I saw you yesterday, when I was inside the marsh harrier..." She shook her head, evidently trying to find the right words. "Animals can perceive things. They are attuned to the afterlife and its death magicks with a keener sense than we credit them with."

"I have no trouble in believing that."

"When I was flying towards you, there was something in the harrier, something intrinsic that was... I don't know. Like a warning. He didn't want to go near the lighthouse."

"I noticed none of the pyracantha berries had been taken. And there were some scraps in the hall which I would have expected rats to carry off."

August nodded. "The local wildlife is frightened of it."

Vonvalt clacked his tongue. "Something to think about."

"Something to think about indeed. Now; if you will excuse me, I shall retire."

"You are not staying here, tonight?"

She smiled. "Not tonight. I need rest."

Vonvalt concealed his disappointment well. "Good evening, then."

"Good evening, Konrad."

V
THE ACCUSED

"The accused must not only be shielded from the capriciousness of the commonfolk and the burdens of institutional oppression, but also from himself. Facing him is the strong arm of the State, the full might of the civic apparatus—being the sole executor of lawful capital punishment. A person so positioned will say almost anything to escape immediate unpleasantness—at the expense of a sturdier, more robust defence in the long term."

—From Caterhauser's *The Sovan Criminal Code: Advice to Practitioners*

THE NEXT MORNING they went to see Havener. By now every last person in Gdansburg knew who they were and the purpose of their visit, and they were watched wherever they went.

They entered the gaol and walked briskly to the end where Havener's cell was. The man was lying down in the corner, facing away from them. He had eaten the food they had provided—grudgingly, Vonvalt imagined—but Havener was still a human being with human needs, and nine times out of ten pride yielded to hunger.

"Sir Bronislav," Vonvalt said, clearing his throat impatiently. When the man did not stir, he rapped on the cell bars. "Sir Bronislav!"

"Piss off," the man grumbled.

"I have some questions for you."

"Fuck your questions."

Vonvalt exchanged a glance with August. "I have Justice Lady August with me."

"Wonderful."

"She will act as an impartial witness."

Havener muttered several oaths into the bed of straw. "An impartial witness to *what*?"

"Your questioning."

Now Havener pressed himself up, and shambled towards the door. "You are not permitted to question me."

Vonvalt's brow furrowed. "I am not sure on what basis you assert that."

Havener made a noise that sounded initially like he was coughing or choking, but became a long, bitter, rattling laugh. "A Justice questioning another Justice? I've never heard of such a thing."

Vonvalt remained stony faced. "Might I suggest then, Justice, a trip back to the Grand Lodge? It seems you are out of touch with the latest procedural rules."

Havener's caustic laughter cut off abruptly. He brandished a finger at Vonvalt through the bars. "Listen to me you upstart—"

"No," August cut in. "It's time for you to listen to us. There's a dead child in this town, and every man jack believes you to be responsible. If you ever want to see the outside of this cell again, I strongly recommend you tell us what happened here."

Havener looked between the three of them. "Who the hell are you?"

"This is Dubine Bressinger, my taskman," Vonvalt said. "He'll be taking a note of what we discuss."

"He hasn't a quill. Or ink. Or paper."

Bressinger tapped the side of his head. "It's a mental note."

Havener sighed. "What's stopping me from remaining silent?"

"Nothing at all, save that I am entitled to draw negative inferences from your silence."

Havener sneered. "Negative inferences?"

"A person innocent of a crime is normally at pains to explain how and why. A person who chooses not to answer might be *inferred* to not *have* any answers that do not inculpate them."

"Look at you, lecturing me as though I were an initiate."

"Sir, if you do not wish to be lectured like an initiate, then do not act like one." Before Havener could angrily rejoin, Vonvalt ploughed on. "Osgar Erikson. The name of the young boy who was killed. What happened to him? Why does everybody in Gdansburg hold you responsible for his death?"

"I don't know."

Vonvalt waited for more, but there was nothing.

"What do you mean, you 'don't know'?"

"Does that have some special meaning in your native Jägeland that I'm not aware of?" Havener snapped. "I mean, *I*, do *not*, *know*. I do not have knowledge of the thing you are asking me."

Vonvalt gritted his teeth. "You were present at the time of his death."

"A great many people were. Question them."

"What happened? Was the boy struck?"

"No. Nothing happened to him. He just started screaming at me. Braying like a donkey, over and over again. Staring at me with his… stupid little eyes."

Vonvalt exchanged a look again with August.

"The boy is dead."

"Aye."

"You do not seem to be unhappy about that."

"Is that what you have inferred? Is that one of your negative inferences?"

"Perhaps I can suggest it is generally accepted that children, especially those with mental defects, are to be afforded greater levels of patience and tolerance."

"Even when they land you in gaol?"

"Even then."

"Says the man standing on the other side of the door."

"Sir Bronislav, the means to secure your release live with you. *Cooperate* with me. Help me understand what has happened, and I shall set you free."

"I don't know what to tell you, Sir Konrad. The boy clapped eyes on me in the middle of the day in a busy street. He screamed at me, over and over again, at the top of his lungs. Everyone was looking at me like I was some sort of leper."

"Who was he with?"

"His parents, who else? The lad was about six years old."

"He was not accompanied by anybody except them?"

"That bitch matria was there. She has it in for me."

"Why?"

"Because she thinks I killed the boy. She was the first to accuse me of murder. Said I had used my 'witchcraft' on him."

"Did you?"

"Did I what?"

"Use your witchcraft on him."

"Do not be ridiculous," Havener snapped. "What could I possibly have done? In broad daylight? With dozens of witnesses?"

"What indeed?"

Havener scoffed.

"Sir Bronislav, why was the boy screaming at you?" August asked.

He shrugged.

"You have no inkling whatever?"

"No."

"He just… looked at you and began screaming?"

"Yes."

"What were you doing in the street?" Vonvalt asked.

"Minding my own bloody business."

"You are here on your circuit?"

"Of course. Why else would I be here?"

"Well, because I am here on my circuit," Vonvalt continued, "and normally the Magistratum is better at spacing us out."

"And yet, here we are. Three Justices, in one tiny, dying, provincial merchant town." Havener shrugged. "The clerks don't always get it right."

"Where are your effects?"

Havener paused. "What?"

"Where are your effects? Your ledgers, warrants of office, seals, volumes of precedent, et cetera."

Havener for the first time seemed slightly flustered. "What do you mean?"

"What do you not understand about the question?"

Havener gave him a vicious look. "They are around somewhere."

"Where? We will secure them for you. They will contain sensitive materials."

"I don't remember."

Vonvalt pulled an expression as though someone had waved a bag of shit under his nose. "You don't remember?"

"Are you just going to repeat everything I say?"

"Sir Bronislav… I find it extraordinary that you cannot recall where you left your belongings."

"They've probably been stolen anyway."

"Stolen from where?" August asked.

"I told you, I don't recall the name of it!"

There was a pause.

"Did you attend to any of the townsfolk's complaints?" Vonvalt asked.

"Of course I did."

"You did?"

"Of course. It was the first thing I did when I arrived."

Now Vonvalt shared a glance with Bressinger.

"Why are you looking at him?" Havener demanded.

"Because, my lord Justice, we ourselves had plenty of complaints to deal with. I did not get the impression that the townsfolk's legal needs had been met. Did you get that impression, Dubine?"

"I didn't get that impression, no."

"No."

Havener folded his arms. "I see. They've got to you. They've poisoned your minds against me. You've spoken to the matria, I take it."

"Of course," Vonvalt said. "A very serious accusation has been levelled against you. Naturally I wanted to understand the situation. Not that anybody seems to be particularly interested in apprising me."

"Because there is nothing to be apprised of. The boy was mentally deficient. He got frightened by me and began screaming, and was so frightened his heart gave out. And now here I am, languishing in this cell, facing a charge of murder. Of a child! For Nema's sake, Sir Konrad, why on earth would I come to this pisswater town and kill a young boy? In the middle of the street? In the middle of the *day*!?"

Vonvalt considered matters. As much as he hated to admit it, Havener was right. It didn't make a scrap of sense. And yet the man was so disagreeable, and the townsfolk so assured of his crime, that he was still loath to release him.

"I'll have more questions for you soon," Vonvalt muttered.

"You know I should be released," Havener called after him as he turned to leave. "You are not permitted to detain me here indefinitely! The criminal procedure rules forbid it!"

"So you remember them when it suits you?" Bressinger called back.

"Dubine," Vonvalt warned.

"What? Fucking prick."

"Come on," August said. "Let's talk outside."

THE THREE OF them moved through Gdansburg down to the old wharf, and there walked along the waterside. Here gulls filled the sky with their shrieking and doused the mooring posts with their guano, and the air smelt strongly of seaweed and brine. Out on the Meridian Ocean, a few fishing vessels shouldered their way through the chop.

"What do you make of it?" Vonvalt asked them.

"I think he's guilty of something," Bressinger muttered, having plucked a small onion from his pocket and taken a bite of it. He spat some sinew out on to the wharf.

"I am stumped by it."

"The great Sir Konrad has finally met his match," August said. "Think of what the pundits will say in Sova."

"Havener has never suffered a particularly vexed reputation, at least not that I can think of," Vonvalt said.

August shrugged. "No, nor I. But he is a member of that old guard, isn't he? Sovan before there was much of a Sovan Empire. He doesn't like us provincials diluting the pool."

"That he does not," Vonvalt said darkly, looking out across the water. "We need to find out more about this lad, and the instigation of his mental deficiency. And the death of the sheriff." He rubbed his chin. "The two seem to have happened at the same time, more or less."

"The 'first time'," August added.

"Yes."

They walked on in silence for a little while. Behind them, the lighthouse loomed on the end of the headland, a morose pinnacle, empty and dark.

"At the same time the haunting began," Vonvalt added after a while.

They all looked at it now, that shabby, crumbling fastness.

"You think there is a connexion?"

"I think a lot of things happened here two years ago," Vonvalt said eventually. He looked up at the sky. It was warm, but the clouds were closing in, and it was getting gloomy. "We need to find out what happened to the sheriff's records. If Matria Klement is now running the place, it stands to reason that she has them."

"Or she burned them," Bressinger said.

"I don't know why she would bother. Klement certainly has it in for Sir Bronislav, but I do not think she is some sort of criminal mastermind. She has been running the abbey—and latterly this town—for two years. I think she has had more than enough legitimate business on her plate without loading it up with illegitimate business as well."

"Or perhaps it is Klement who you should be investigating," August said. "She seems mightily keen to pin this slaying on Havener."

"The thought had crossed my mind," Vonvalt murmured. "Which I am keeping open for now."

"I shall have a look in the abbey tonight," Bressinger said. "See if I can turn up anything."

Vonvalt nodded. "Let us hope it yields fruit." He turned back to the ocean, thinking. "Unfortunately Havener is right. We are going to have to either charge him, or turn him loose in the next day or two."

"If there's something to be found, I'll find it," Bressinger said.

"I know you will, Dubine. Come; let us find some lunch."

✦

THE THREE OF them returned to the Brass Wyvern that evening, and Vonvalt and August retired to his bedchamber.

Bressinger had a few hours to kill, and took the time to sample a few of the local delights. This took the form of a buxom woman who doubled as one of the serving maids, though there was nothing maidlike about her.

"How do you want it?" she asked after he had paid. She had taken him to a pokey little room, all straw and low-hanging beams, which was directly over the common hearth such that it was sweltering hot.

"Give us a go on those beauties," he said, reclining on the bed, and she unloaded the largest pair of breasts he'd ever seen into his waiting hands.

"You're like a lad," she said. "All fumbling and squeezing and—ah!—pinching."

"Aye, well," Bressinger chuckled. "You never grow out of your love of 'em."

"I'll say." She reached a practised hand down to his groin and began fumbling his balls like a bag of coins. "What next?"

"Bloody Nema, got somewhere to be, have you?"

She actually yawned. "No."

He sighed. "Just hands tonight. Got something the matter."

She looked down at his cock. "Looks alright to me."

He closed his eyes and lay back, and she spent the better part of ten minutes tugging as though he were a water pump. She changed hands several times as her wrists grew tired, and at least once Bressinger felt a bead of sweat land on him. It really was hot in that room.

Eventually matters reached their inevitable end, and she wiped her hands off.

"All done, then?" she asked, tucking her breasts back into her kirtle.

"Mm," he muttered, profoundly unsatisfied. "Here, answer me a question."

"Questions cost extra."

"You should be paying me after that performance!"

"The bloody cheek on you!"

"Listen. How do you find the matria? Klement."

"She's in the abbey most days."

"Not literally," Bressinger said patiently. "I mean, what's she like? As master of Gdansburg."

The woman shrugged. "As good as any, I suppose. She looks after us."

"She seems like a hotheaded woman."

"Aye, no question of that."

"Do you have any notion of what happened with the Justice?"

She blew out her lips. "I wasn't there for it. I've probably heard as much about it as you have."

"What about the old sheriff?"

"What about him?"

"Why isn't he running the place?"

"Apart from his being dead?"

"Aye. Apart from that."

"Are you serious?"

"What was he like? Old? Infirm? Did he have any plans to retire that you knew of?"

She thought a moment. "No. No to all of it. He was older than me, but not a day over sixty."

"Not ill?"

"No. He was still busy keeping order when he passed. In fact I think he had only just started looking into the Osgar Erikson matter when his heart gave out."

Bressinger managed to conceal his surprise at that. "Oh aye?"

She nodded. "Aye. Lad lost his wits, didn't he. They took him up to the abbey after. He became too unruly for his parents. Screaming and shouting all sorts of nonsense. They kept him in the orphanage there with the other waifs. There were a lot more of them back then."

"Why did he lose his wits?"

"No one knows. Anyway, after the business with the lighthouse, the town emptied out, and everybody just sort of… moved on."

"Except the lad's parents."

"Aye. And Radmila. She took it very hard. She's like a second mother to that boy. Was."

"Tell me; what happened to the sheriff?"

"I said; his heart gave out. A day or two later. They found him in his office."

"What happened to all his papers and the like?"

"Oh all of that stuff went up to the abbey."

Bressinger affected nonchalance. "Kept them all, did they?"

"Certainly did. He had so many ledgers, they had to use a mule and cart to transport them into the crypts. He was a careful record keeper. We all used to make fun of him for being a 'good Sovan'. 'Twas the Imperials after all who made him do it. Always writing he was. He was a good man. He taught all his deputies to read and write as well. Insisted on it."

The evening had taken a maudlin turn, but Bressinger had everything he needed.

"Go on then," he said, nodding to the door. "You can be about your evening."

She scoffed. "If by 'be about my evening' you mean go to bed, then certainly. 'Tis nearly the eleventh bell."

Bressinger watched her leave, pretending to prepare for sleep.

A LITTLE WHILE later, just before midnight, he was moving through

Gdansburg clad in dark clothing. He kept to the coastline. It was the much more treacherous route: ink black, slippery, beset by small cliffs, seaweed slime, and the clutches of the midnight tide; but it had the great benefit of being utterly devoid of people.

Gdansburg was the same as every other settlement Bressinger could call to mind except Sova; the life cycle of the town followed the sun, which meant long days and hard work in summer and short, dreary ones in winter. In those latter, colder months, most would rise for an hour or two in the dead of night, and read, or pray, and sometimes eat. But here on the west coast, in summer, it wasn't fully dark until gone the tenth bell, and most people would now sleep the night through.

Or so he hoped.

It was a cloudy night, with little moonlight. He made his way north, picking through the rock pools and pebbles and sand and grit, until he reached the low headland upon which sat the abbey. Most of these old gothick klosters, especially ones abutting the sea, had secret accesses. They were built, over the centuries, for a variety of reasons—for the inhabitants to escape marauding pagans, or in the case of ascetics, for the matrias and patrias to engage in illicit sexual affairs. When he found it, it was clear that this one had been built for the purposes of smuggling.

"Here we go," he muttered. It looked like a cave, or a natural point of saltwater erosion in the cliffside, rather than a tunnel. But on entry, he realised that it was indeed a deliberate passageway, just one so eroded by the Meridian and overgrown with barnacles that it appeared natural.

Inside was the detritus of a once-burgeoning smuggling operation. The place opened up to a broad chamber, one that had been buttressed with barrel vaulting, and was filled with old casks and crates, most rotted beyond use. Had he had more time, and a little more light, he would have investigated further. But even with Bressinger's keen night vision, the place was as black as pitch, and he had to feel his way carefully through it.

He walked headlong into an iron ladder. He spent a few moments swearing and rubbing his forehead; then he ascended. At the top was a trapdoor, held shut by an ancient, rusted padlock, and he spent a quarter-hour laboriously oiling and picking it.

He opened the trapdoor and quietly climbed into the bowels of the abbey. This was another barrel vault hewn out of the cliff rock, a drier storeroom where both in- and outgoing illicit goods had been kept. He felt his way through it, and to another locked door which he picked open.

Now it was simply a question of locating the crypt. Most Neman klosters were constructed in the same way—because most of them were converted centuries-old pagan klosters, where the inhabitants worshipped the deer-headed god 'Oleni' rather than the Sovan deer-headed god 'Nema'. He moved quickly and quietly through the lowest parts of the abbey, constantly pausing and listening out for movement, but there was nothing. The place, like the town, was mostly empty.

Eventually he found the crypt, a musty space filled with old bones. Sure enough, stacked up at one end were piles of strongboxes, heaps of ledgers, scrolls, and other paraphernalia. Now he had no choice but to light a small pocket candle, and cupped his hand around the flame. He rifled through some of the books. None were from the sheriff's office. Plenty were agricultural and tax records, grain store ledgers, and other administrative accounts—stacks of them, some on vellum, some on ancient scrolls, more still on modern paper.

Bressinger was a talented infiltrator, and had undertaken the task many times in Vonvalt's service, but even he began to get antsy after a quarter-hour of fruitless searching.

"Come *on*," he whispered.

He was about to give up when he uncovered a strongbox marked with the Sovan device: the two-headed wolf of House Haugenate. He prised it open, and found several loose sheets inside, as well as a dozen thick leather ledgers, each embossed with the same device. Bressinger recognised them immediately; these were the volumes that Justices carried around with them and handed out to provincial lawkeepers to record crimes.

He opened the first one, which by coincidence was the most recent—though it was two years old.

Then he paused.

He shielded the candle from an errant gust of cold air. He looked over to the door. Was that a flicker of light, or had he imagined it? He stood in total silence and stillness for a hundred heartbeats, straining to hear. But there was nothing except the wash of the tide where it fizzed and bubbled around the foot of the cliffs.

He returned to the ledger, and flicked to the final entries. There was a scrap of paper acting as a bookmark there. He unfolded it. Written in shaky, spidery gothick script were the words:

What is the Scour?

"What is the Scour?" Bressinger whispered. Then he paused again. There was another noise, and it was not the wash of brine against rock. It was the unmistakable scuff of a human extremity against stone.

His heart leapt. He turned back to the ledger, and quickly read the final entries:

12 SORPEN *{34. Anno imperii Sovi}*	*H. Dahl held for petty larceny.* *Stockade 1 hr.* *Brother arrested for interference in spite warning. 5x lash.*
15 SORPEN *{34. Anno imperii Sovi}*	*Kjeld Danielsen affray.* *Stockade 1 hr.*
17 SORPEN *{34. Anno imperii Sovi}*	*Osgar Erikson attended sheriff's office w/ parents.* *Lad v frightened.* *Seen something - marsh?* *Boy insensible.*
17 SORPEN *{34. Anno imperii Sovi}*	*Lissi Vang elopement w/ Dennish deserter. 2 men dispatched to retrieve but too far gone. Family to seek reparations/dowry??*

Bressinger looked up sharply. There was someone at the crypt door. He blew out the candle, and stuffed the papers he held into his pocket. But it was too late. He had been seen.

"You there!" shouted a man in that strange Brigalander-accented Grozodan. He had his own torch, and behind him, Bressinger saw several more men wearing habits. They were all armed with cudgels.

"Shit," Bressinger said, ripping off the top few pages of the ledger and pocketing them, too. Then he darted past the men, and through the door at the far end of the chamber. Behind him they shouted incoherently and gave chase. Now there was an undignified scramble through the chambers he had passed on his way in, and then through the trapdoor and down the ladder into the smugglers' cave. The tide had risen, so that the frigid, brackish water was at midcalf.

"Get back here!" the men bellowed behind him.

Bressinger waded his way south along the coast and then exited the ocean and clambered across the rocks, chafing and cutting his hands and shins. They stung with the saltwater.

"Fucking hell," he grumbled as he turned and saw the men still following him. There were a sizeable number of them, perhaps a dozen or so. This was no chance encounter.

He pushed through the westernmost extremity of Gdansburg and then on to the second headland, now running at full tilt to where the abandoned lighthouse stood. Its broken stone tower was black against the deep purple of the ocean night.

He paused only very briefly at the threshold of the curtain wall, before he pushed into the empty courtyard, and then into the old keep itself.

And there, he waited.

He heard the men—and dogs, now, too—approach a little while later.

"We know you're in there," one of them called out.

Bressinger heard the dogs whine.

"Go on boy, go and get him," another of the men urged.

The dogs whined again.

"Bloody useless hound!"

"You go in then!"

"I'm not going in that cursed place."

Bressinger waited as the men moved around the outside of the courtyard. When it became clear that none of them would cross the threshold, he sat down, and rested his back against the cold stone wall. A place like this, abandoned and open to anyone who cared to enter, should have been festooned with animals—gulls, shanks, pipers, herons—to say nothing of the foxes and rats, wild cats and dogs, and asps. But there was nothing. No movement at all.

Eventually the posse lost interest, or at least stopped making noise. Now Bressinger began to think seriously about how he was going to get away. He couldn't wait until dawn, for it was likely they would take some courage from daylight and rush the place. He certainly couldn't go back out the way he had come. It seemed his only choice was to try and find an exit much like the one in the abbey, or to scale the cliffs themselves. Neither option seemed attractive.

And then, at some point after the third bell, something began to shuffle through the darkened keep.

"Nema preserve me," he whispered.

He was pressed into a corner, so much so that if he pushed any harder he would make himself part of the wall. He peered into the gloom, trying to make out what it was that was approaching. But the darkness had taken on a tangible quality—not merely the absence of light, but a thick, oil-black cloud, spreading out to fill the hall.

Bressinger was a brave man, but he was also just that—a man. He hadn't the minerals for this.

"Whoever you are, leave me alone," he said. His voice crashed with appalling volume off the hard surfaces of the castle. "I mean you no ill will."

And then his blood froze in his veins, and his heart stuck fast in his chest, for someone was holding his arm, and there were lips brushing against his ear, and he could smell the familiar corpse-stink of decay in his nostrils.

"Look to the Scour," whispered a woman in his ear, and then Bressinger was screaming like a little boy, and the apparition was screaming a horrible, bloodcurdling banshee keen, and he was running out of that place at full tilt, and his would-be captors were all screaming and running as well, all of them screaming like frightened children, any enmity forgotten in their mad, thoughtless desperation to get away from that hellish place.

VI
SHEDDING BLOOD

"Killing a person is often considered the greatest crime of all, but of course there are circumstances in which even the wickedest offences are perfectly justifiable. A man may bereave two-dozen families if he is acting in lawful self-defence."

—From Caterhauser's *The Sovan Criminal Code: Advice to Practitioners*

RIGHT," VONVALT SAID, sweeping into the common room and bringing with him a vortex of damp morning air. "Let's have it."

August and Bressinger looked up from their breakfast. His taskman looked terrible, his eyes bloodshot, his skin still sallow and hanging off him ghoulishly. Vonvalt doubted sleep would find the man for some days yet.

"Again?" Bressinger asked miserably.

Vonvalt took out his pipe, packed it, and lit it. He smoked thoughtfully for a few moments. "Again. Now that you've had a chance to calm down."

The night had been an eventful one. A group of half a dozen men clad in Neman habits and with two large plains mastiffs had torn through Gdansburg sometime after the third bell, and sent up such a clamour that, as Vonvalt had surfaced to wakefulness, he'd thought the place under attack from a marauding band.

Thereafter he and August had joined a large and growing number of townsfolk in the streets, and had intercepted his taskman, who had given a garbled, nonsensical account of spirits in the lighthouse, of hauntings, and of something he had repeatedly referred to as 'the Scour'. Eventually, they had taken him back to the Brass Wyvern, where he had been plied with alcohol and sat down. Even then, after much patient probing, nothing useful had been drawn from him.

Vonvalt had spent the next couple of hours tracking down and collaring the posse of men who had been chasing, and latterly fleeing with, Bressinger. They told him they had been summoned by one of the nuns in the abbey after a suspected break-in, had found his taskman poking around in the crypts, and had chased him to the lighthouse. There they had all heard a supernatural screaming, and, overcome, had fled.

These sorts of goings-on tended to annoy Vonvalt more than anything else. But it was rare for Bressinger to be so affected, and in view of August's warning about the lighthouse—and his own misgivings, which he trusted over and above anything else—he was prepared to take this seriously.

"I found the sheriff's records, as you instructed," Bressinger said. He stopped then, as a thought seemed to occur to him. "Nema, the papers."

Vonvalt and August waited as Bressinger disappeared upstairs to his lodgings, and returned with several torn, wet, and wadded-up sheets of paper. "I tried to keep them dry. I… don't think I've succeeded."

"What are these?" Vonvalt asked as he accepted the papers. He began to carefully unfold them.

"They were in the sheriff's ledger. I read what I could by candle-light."

"What did it say?"

"That the boy had been taken by his parents to the sheriff to report a crime. That he had seen something in the marsh, and had been frightened by it. The very next entry was a line about how the boy had lost his mind. And then there was this note tucked into the pages. It said, 'what is the Scour?'"

Vonvalt observed a curious effect in his taskman then. He seemed to be completely overcome. He struggled to speak for a few moments; then he actually began to weep.

"Dubine," August said tenderly, putting her arm around him. She looked up at Vonvalt. "Whatever is in that place, we cannot leave here without remedying it."

Vonvalt shook his head. "Seems to me they need an exorcist, not a Justice."

He finally succeeded in prising open the papers. They were wet, but the paper had been well made, and the ink was not too badly smudged. He read through the ledger's final entries, and then the piece of paper with the reference to 'the Scour' on it. "The sheriff wrote this, did he?"

Bressinger nodded. "The girl in the lighthouse mentioned it too. 'Look to the Scour'."

"I wonder what it is," Vonvalt murmured.

"Perhaps it was responsible for Osgar's malady," August offered.

"That was my thought too." Then Vonvalt peeled back the folded pages of the final sheet Bressinger had taken. "Oh," he said.

"What?" August asked. "Konrad, what?"

"I think I have just found a very large missing piece of the puzzle."

"What? What is it?"

"Come on," he said, turning and sweeping towards the door.

The three of them moved through the main thoroughfares of Gdansburg until they reached the town gaol. Before they entered, Vonvalt turned to them. "You spoke about the 'first time', yes? That the boy had not been the same, mentally, since the 'first time'?"

"Yes, I remember."

Vonvalt held up the wet piece of paper. "It was the first time Havener was here. Here is a note from the sheriff's office, confirming it."

They stood in silence a moment. "You mean to say he has been here before?" August asked.

"Let me guess," Bressinger said. "Two years ago."

Vonvalt pointed at him. "Correct."

"By Nema," August said. "What is going *on*?"

"Believe me, Resi, I intend to find out," Vonvalt said, and opened the door. They moved down the corridor, to the now-familiar cell at the end of the row. "Sir Bronislav," Vonvalt said, pulling back the shutter over the barred window. "Sir B—"

He stopped.

Havener was gone.

"KONRAD, WHAT ARE you going to do?"

Vonvalt swept towards the abbey, his fury radiating off him.

"Konrad?" August pressed, a warning note in her voice.

"At this rate, Resi, I'm going to hang the lot of them."

"They can't have gone far—" Bressinger began.

"I care not how far they have gone!" Vonvalt exploded. "I care that they have gone at all!"

The townsfolk gathered to watch this impressive trio of Imperials moving through the public spaces of Gdansburg. There were not a few guilty looks being thrown their way.

"This whole bloody town conspires against me," Vonvalt muttered. "I've half a mind to turn Havener loose out of spite."

"If he still draws breath," Bressinger said.

"If they have killed him, I will burn this place to the ground."

"It's a funny thing, is it not? The man may well die, either by our hand or theirs. But when they do it, 'tis murder."

"They are not clothed in the Emperor's authority," August said.

"Can the pair of you shut up?" Vonvalt snapped.

"You can talk to him like that, Konrad, but I am not your subordinate," August replied.

"Thank you for that, Resi," Bressinger said. He looked as though he were about to say more, but instead his eye was drawn to the headland upon which the abbey sat. There, a group of men—amongst whom stood, doubtless, some of those who had chased Bressinger the night before—barred the way to the entrance.

"What is the meaning of this?" Vonvalt demanded, though the meaning was as plain as the sun in the sky.

"We will not permit you to harm the matria," the foremost man said. He and the others wielded an assortment of melee weapons.

Vonvalt turned to August. "Are you armed?" he asked, but already his eyes had found the Sovan short sword buckled about her hips. He turned back to the posse. "Listen to me very carefully," he said. "Justice Sir Bronislav Havener is an Imperial Magistrate. He is also a Sovan citizen and subject, as are all of you. This means that he, and everybody else within the bounds of the Empire, must, as a matter of law, submit to my authority."

"Get fucked, Imperial."

"I am not in the habit of repeating myself, nor of issuing idle threats. So I shall say this one time only. After that, it will be the noose for all of you."

The foremost man scoffed, but he was alone in this. Already his fellows were looking nervous.

"I am investigating Justice Havener for the crime of murder. He is subject to the same laws as anybody else. His being an Imperial Magistrate does not put him beyond my reach, nor the reach of my colleagues here. It also does not put him beyond the reach of a lawfully constituted lawkeeper's office operating under the auspices of a sheriff with an Imperial warrant." Vonvalt brandished a finger. "What it *does* do, is put him beyond the reach of *you*."

"Yeah? Tell that to—"

"Shut the fuck up!" Bressinger snapped, and the man did.

"What you are now doing," Vonvalt continued, "in taking him away, without commission, is the crime of vigilantism." There was a pause. The ocean breeze cut between them like an apologetic bystander. "I'm setting this all out very clearly, do you understand? So that you all fully understand the consequences of refusing to assist me."

The man at the head of the posse spat on the ground. His grip tightened around the cudgel he wielded. "We will not permit—"

"Permit? *Permit*! It is not your business to permit anything whatever! You are lucky to still be breathing! Now, get out of my way, all of you."

"Stay where you are!" the man shouted.

"Last chance," August said softly. "Anyone who leaves now will not face punishment."

"By Nema they shall!" Vonvalt scoffed.

"Sir Konrad," August said in his ear. "If you—"

Vonvalt's brow furrowed as she let out a strange sound, a sort of surprised grunt, and shoved past him. A moment later, something hot and wet splashed against his face, something with the smell of soil and iron.

"Resi?" Vonvalt breathed, pulse pounding and wide-eyed, as a wretched, gurgling sound filled the air—alongside a great foreign clamouring. He touched his face and neck, where blood showered him. "Resi!"

His hand went to the hilt of his sword. There, in front of him, the man stood clutching his throat. August's short sword was stuck into it four inches deep, and the man's hands were wrapped around the blade. It was a phenomenon Vonvalt had seen many times in the Reichskrieg: men instinctively grabbing swords after a failed parry, cutting open their hands, incurring permanent muscle and tendon damage—and more often than not losing them altogether—to prevent the steel penetrating their vital organs.

August withdrew the weapon, sawing open the man's neck as far back as his spinal bone so that his head flopped backwards. On the floor in front of him was a dropped dagger, and suddenly the scene and commotion made sense.

The man collapsed to the floor soundlessly. The men behind him looked aghast. One of them was sick. The rest stared, sallow and sweating, with no stomach whatever for these violent intrigues. Vonvalt had thought they might have leapt forward, roused to sudden, ferocious retribution. Instead their blood turned to water.

August wiped her blade off on a cloth and slid it into its scabbard. She looked very unhappy.

"And now he is dead," she said.

"Just so," Vonvalt muttered, eyeing the corpse. "What a fool."

Somewhere off to the left, back in the town, a woman was screaming.

"The rest of you fuck off," Bressinger shouted at the gaggle of would-be lynchers, and they did, skittering away across the compacted earth like whipped dogs.

"I've half a mind to charge Klement with manslaughter," Vonvalt said, looking up at the abbey.

August sighed angrily. "You really think that is the solution do you?"

Vonvalt looked at her. She was trembling slightly where her heart was pounding. He wondered when she had last killed someone.

"No," he said eventually, his eyes tracing the line of the lighthouse, and then the coast, and then back to the abbey. The woman in Gdansburg was still screaming, doubtless the dead man's wife, or beau. Well, if he hadn't wanted to die, he shouldn't have tried to murder an Imperial Justice.

"Come on," Vonvalt said. "Let's get on with it."

KLEMENT WAS IN her office overlooking the ocean, and seemed both genuinely surprised and frightened to see them.

"You have cost a man his life," Vonvalt said as they entered. "I might see that you pay for it with yours."

"What happened?" she demanded, but gone was the belligerence. Now she looked like a frail old woman, in over her head.

"You mean to tell us you were not watching through the keyhole?" August said.

Klement swallowed. "You murdered—"

"But it was not murder! Was it, Matria?" Vonvalt interrupted. "It was an illegal assembly of men attempting to interfere with the lawful business of a Justice. If I had my way—and I still might, against the urgent counsel of my colleagues—every one of them would be hanging this evening. And the man who lies dead outside this kloster, Ms Klement, tried to slay me. Doubtless at your instigation."

"No," Klement said sharply, looking profoundly alarmed. "No! I was insistent there was to be no violence. I was explicit. The others will attest."

"Oh, we shall be checking in with them later, fret not." Vonvalt pulled out a chair and sat on it. August did the same; Bressinger remained standing. "It is time to make a clean breast of things, Matria.

You have obstructed and obfuscated since we arrived." Klement opened her mouth to speak, but Vonvalt held up a hand for silence, then pointed behind him. "One of those men made the mistake of doubting me, Matria. And now look at him. He lies on the dirty ground, his life extinguished on a random autumn afternoon, for absolutely no reason at all. Do not think you are beyond the same."

Her expression curdled. "I'll help you, Imperial."

"I know," Vonvalt said, relighting his pipe and smoking it. He reclined in his seat. "Tell me everything. Including where you have taken Sir Bronislav."

Klement sighed. Her obstreperousness left her so fully that it seemed to exit her like a cloud of vapour.

"This is not the first time Justice Havener has come to Gdansburg."

"We know."

"Worked it out from the stolen documents, did you?"

Vonvalt cast a brief glance over to Bressinger. "Something like that."

"He came around two years ago. Much like yourselves, swanning into the place, all piss and vinegar. Thought he was better than all of us. This was back when the town was busy of course, so there was lots of business for him. Lots of trade disputes. Men and women from the wharf, all clamouring to avail themselves of the *Emperor's Justice*. He was a busy man for several days." She spoke with venom. "And then… something happened. With Osgar Erikson."

"What happened?"

"That's what I've been trying to find out, Justice. We didn't really put two and two together until earlier this week, when he returned. The way the lad just screamed at him, like he had seen a ghost."

"Why do you think that has anything to do with Sir Bronislav?"

"It's the *timing* of it. It's all too much of a coincidence. Havener came here two years ago. The day before he left, Osgar Erikson had seen something. He'd spoken to the sheriff about it. He was terrified. The boy had gone white as White Nema. Erik and Freya tried to draw him out, to try and get him to speak, but the lad had been turned simple overnight. No sign of a blow to the head. Something had frightened him out of his wits." Klement shook her head. "After that… he couldn't think. Couldn't speak. Just… sat there, staring. It was that or raging. We cared for him in the orphanage as often as we could." She sighed. "And then everything else started going wrong. Strange goings-on in the lighthouse. Horrible screaming at night. You know the rest; no one would go in to light it, and then the wrecks, and the dissolution of Gdansburg as a port." Vonvalt watched her hands bunch into fists. "Now he's come back again, and set the lad off screaming until his little heart gave up on it all. It was bad enough, losing him the first time. Prince of Hell, some would say his death was a mercy. But not me. And certainly not Freya and Erik. They loved that little boy, and I did too. And Havener took him from us. *Twice.* He must face punishment, Sir Konrad." Now she looked at him with wide, watery eyes. "He *must* have a reckoning. He cannot get away with it simply because he is a Justice."

"Madam, I can assure you that his being a Justice has no bearing whatever on his culpability, nor on the punishment he will face. Merely the process and the procedure by which we bring it about, but I need not burden you with that. That is something for me and Justice Lady August to concern ourselves with." He was silent for a few moments, smoking thoughtfully. "Tell me something."

"What?"

"What is the Scour?"

Klement had such a visceral reaction to the words that Vonvalt actually thought she had died. She sat there in shocked stillness, eyes wide, breath fading to nothingness. It got to the point where Vonvalt thought the words carried with them some arcane quality, and that simply by uttering them he had slain her.

"Where did you hear about the Scour?" she asked, her voice barely breath.

"It was written in the sheriff's logbook."

"His what?"

"His logbook. The ones you were keeping here. In the crypts."

She shook her head, agape. Her hand went to her mouth. It was shaking. "So he had heard it too."

Vonvalt glanced at Bressinger, but the man seemed to be all right. "We think it might be something to do with the lighthouse."

"It is," the matria said, still whispering. "I think so." She nodded. "I think it is."

Vonvalt leant forward. "Seems like the boy was frightened too. Out of his wits. Do you think it could be this… spirit? This haunting?"

"Could be," Klement said. She seemed insensible. "Could be."

"Madam, you seem frightened, for want of a better word. Would you mind explaining what it is that has you so worked up?"

Klement took a deep breath. "A little while after the lighthouse was first… *claimed*, the townsfolk asked me to go in. Burn some sage, say some prayers. Exorcise the place." She seemed to notice Vonvalt's pipe for the first time. "May I?"

"Certainly," Vonvalt said, and offered his little leather pouch of leaf. She withdrew some, thumbed it into a pipe which she took out of a desk drawer, and then lit it from a candle. She smoked for a few moments, letting the leaf calm her nerves.

"Whilst I was in there, someone spoke to me."

"A woman?" Bressinger asked.

Klement nodded, then paused. "How do you know?"

"I heard it too. Last night." He gestured broadly to Gdansburg. "Hence all the bloody screaming. She said—"

"—Look to the Scour."

"Aye."

Vonvalt looked between the pair of them. "What *is* it?"

Klement sighed. "I know not. But I have a theory."

"Which is?"

"Every so often, the town is wracked by a terrible storm. The sort of storm we would once have lit the lighthouse for. And every time this storm comes in, the ocean ploughs into the saltmarsh to the north and cuts great rents into it down to the peat, and smashes up against the cliffs, and overwhelms the sea wall protecting the harbour. It is a vile squall, and I think if it continues we shall have to abandon this place."

"You think that inclement weather is—"

"Oh no, my lord Justice, no no," she said, chuckling darkly. "This is not 'inclement weather'. This is something else. This is *malevolent.*"

"The haunting and the storms are related to one another?"

"Unquestionably. It took me a while to make the connexion. Whenever the storm blows in, the… *arcane activity* becomes worse. People hear screaming. Strange things happen. Scratching on doors, animals spooked, whispers in the night. 'Tis as though whatever ghost lingers in that place, it is carried by the storm into the town. It is not just the loss of trade that has driven people away from here, Sir Konrad. It is the lady of the lighthouse."

As she said it, it sent a thrill of fear through the three of them. The chamber seemed to draw in and darken.

Vonvalt straightened up, shaking his head. "Leaving these matters aside for the moment—"

"Is it true you can speak with the dead?" Klement asked suddenly.

Vonvalt chewed his lip. It was always difficult to know how to broach this subject. In the halls and corridors and warded training chambers of the Magistratum, the matter could be referred to freely, and discussed in practical and academic terms. Out here in the provinces, at the very furthest extent of the Two-Headed Wolf's outstretched claw, it was discussed in hushed, frightened tones—and more likely not at all. To many of the people in Gdansburg, Vonvalt's being a Justice was more akin to being a mage.

"I have certain abilities," he allowed.

He watched, then, as two conflicting emotions performed a familiar dance within her; her intrinsic hatred of him and everything he represented, clashing with her fear, and the fact that she had lost control of the situation—if she'd ever had it. The only person who could help her was the same person whom she detested.

"I fear that whatever Osgar saw drove him mad," Klement continued. "And I fear that it is that thing residing in our lighthouse."

"Have you questioned Justice Havener on this?"

"We have asked Justice Havener many questions, and he has refused to help us at all. Hence..." She gestured vaguely to the north.

"Where have you taken him?" Vonvalt asked gently but firmly. When she hesitated, he said, "Matria, I am here to assist you. To see that justice is done. But I cannot help you if you continue to break the law. You will force my hand."

"I will turn Justice Havener in to your custody after you have looked at the lighthouse," she said, meeting his eye. There was the old fire in her. Even though it was pissing Vonvalt off something ferocious, he had to admire the woman's minerals.

Before he could reply, August laid a hand on his forearm. "May I speak with you?" she asked. "In private."

"Of course. Excuse me, Matria."

He followed August out of the office and into the hallway outside.

"What is it?" he asked.

She looked at him, examining his face, taking in his features. He looked back at her, trying to discern what it was she was going to say. But already he had a pretty good idea. This was Resi August, after all, a woman whom he had known since they were initiates in the Grand

Lodge. And despite their inability to form any sort of long-term commitment, he liked to think he knew her more intimately than anyone else.

"You want to chastise me," he said.

"I do," she said. "You are in need of chastisement."

Vonvalt nodded. "You are probably right."

August nodded in the direction of the town. "We have a chance to do some good here."

"I know."

"Shut up and listen to me a moment."

"All right."

"These places, these people, they hate us. We are walking, breathing embodiments of the nation state. Of Sova. These people are our subjugates in every way that matters. We may as well have personally taken Gdansburg from them."

Vonvalt nodded.

"The greatest threat to the cohesion of the Empire is not armed rebellion. There is nothing on this continent that can best Sova's Legions. It is a failure of will. An absence of belief. I am not so foolish as to believe that slaying tens of thousands in the name of conquest is an objectively good thing, but it has been done now, whether we like it or not. Our task, as Justices, is to make sure that the people who have the most right to hate us are given the least reason to. That *means*," she said, jabbing an index finger into his breastbone, "even-handedness. Fairness. Justice, for everyone, without fear or favour. That the common law is precisely that—*common* to everyone, be they a peasant, or an Imperial Magistrate."

"Resi, with the greatest respect, what is it you think you are teaching me? I know all of this."

"Then *act* like it!" she hissed with sudden fury. "You have spent half a decade in Sova, marinating in its pomp and circumstance, walking the corridors of power, bathing in the respect and adulation of a grateful public and the prostration and fawning of a carousel of senators. You have been at the Emperor's side, trying traitors in great spectacular show trials, and you have lost all sense of deftness, of *nuance.* Yes, of course, we could prosecute and hang Matria Klement for interfering with our investigation, but what good would that do anybody, except lead to the dissolution of Gdansburg and the seething resentment of everyone in it? You expect blind obedience at every turn simply by presenting your person. You rage at these people for not leaping, with alacrity, to your commands like hounds. Whether or not you are entitled to it, do you truly expect them to be grateful for you being here? Especially in the wake of Havener. Truly?"

Vonvalt hated being lectured more than anything else, especially on matters which he considered himself to be intimately familiar with. This was one of those exceedingly rare instances where the person doing the lecturing was someone he happened to both love and respect.

"Fine," he said.

August cocked an eyebrow. "That's it?"

"I'm saying I agree with you."

August looked around, affecting great confusion. "Once more? Sir Konrad? I'm afraid I didn't quite hear that."

"Oh, shut up Resi," Vonvalt muttered, shoving her, and she laughed.

"Now," she said. "I'm going to find out where Havener is. I'll be in my chamber in the Brass Wyvern."

"What is it you expect me to do?"

"Why, Konrad; it sounds to me like you're going to spend the night in the lighthouse."

VII
A NIGHT TO FORGET

"The Justice sits at the nexus of the legal and the arcane. As many an unwary Magistratum initiate will attest, it is often the former that is the more complex, baffling, and frightening."

—From Caterhauser's *The Sovan Criminal Code: Advice to Practitioners*

BEFORE VONVALT DID anything, there was a burden of administration to be taken care of. A man had been killed, after all.

"You are fortunate," Bressinger said as they sat in Vonvalt's chamber. He was holding a half-eaten onion in one hand, and rearranging his package with the other.

"Must you do that here and now?" Vonvalt said with distaste.

"Got a mustard poultice haven't I," he grumbled. "Feels like the only thing that could have made the burning worse."

"What else did the physician tell you?"

"Drink as much boiled water as possible to flush out the toxins. And to avoid alcohol."

"You should listen to him."

"Her."

"You should listen to her."

"I am listening."

"Dubine, I just watched you drink two pints of ale."

Bressinger waved him off.

"If that pox worsens, it will spread to your kidneys, and you will die. Listen to what the physician told you."

"Nema, fine! You missed your calling to the blue star."

"Be quiet. I am trying to work."

Vonvalt bent back over his ledger, and wrote:

03 VANDAHAR *(36. Anno imperii Sovi)*	*Karl Ottosen (47) killed in lawful self defence by J. Lady Resi August whilst attempting to attack J. Sir Konrad Vonvalt with dirk.* *No further action required.*

"Why do you say I am fortunate?"

"Hm?"

Vonvalt set down his quill. "Why do you say I am fortunate?"

"Did I say that?"

"You said it not two minutes ago."

"Oh," Bressinger said. "I meant the man Resi killed. He was not well-liked in the town. Bit of a shit stirrer. Bit of a brawler. Sounds to me like you did them a favour."

"That is fortunate."

"You don't seem to be particularly pleased."

"What have I to be pleased about? I'm about to spend the night alone in a haunted lighthouse."

"I'm glad you said that."

"Said what?"

"'Alone'."

"I should command you to attend me."

"I should stick that command up your arse."

Vonvalt snorted, as did Bressinger.

"Anyway," Bressinger continued. "I thought you didn't believe in that sort of thing."

"It's not a question of belief. These matters are as tangible as you and I."

"That's not what you said before. Back east."

"If the afterlife is a real place that I can visit at will, then it stands to reason that occasionally there will be bleed across the mortal plane and holy dimensions. I've never come across it personally—except at my own instigation—but the weight of evidence is too great to ignore now."

"The great Sir Konrad Vonvalt, finally taking his taskman at his word."

"Yes well," Vonvalt said, standing. "There's a first time for everything."

✦

IT WAS JUST after the eighth bell, and the weather was closing in. As they approached the lighthouse, Vonvalt could see a great black thunderhead sailing across the Meridian Ocean like Death's own corsair.

"Did you ever see anything like it," Bressinger murmured.

"No."

It was a solid wall of cloud, two miles across, racing towards Gdansburg. Lightning flickered and crackled above it, and thunder, distant and much delayed, rumbled across the coast like a rockslide.

"I have a bad feeling about this."

"At least you get to go back to the brothel."

Bressinger shook his head. "No," he sighed with great reluctance. "I shall accompany you."

Vonvalt put a hand on his shoulder. "I'm grateful."

"You had better bloody be."

They moved up the headland towards the lighthouse. To the south, the saltmarsh stretched calmly and glassily, a brackish oasis preparing for the great ocean assault. Vonvalt was aware of many pairs of eyes watching them from the town. Word had spread quickly.

"What is the Scour?" Vonvalt murmured. "I wonder if we shall have our answer tonight."

"I have a feeling we will."

The thunderhead approached with incredible speed now, and the Meridian was being whipped up into great spraying whitecaps. Already they could see from their vantage point waves lapping over the harbour wall.

"A vile squall indeed," Vonvalt said, and walked on.

IT WAS DIFFICULT to know where to go in the castle. But in spite of its crumbling walls and general state of disrepair, the whole point of the building was to withstand such storms as these, and Vonvalt had little compunction in making his way to the top of the tower itself.

Here the wind truly raged. The leading edge of the thunderhead was almost on them now, cutting out what little remained of the evening's gloam, and they were pelted with rain. To the north, Gdansburg pounded with the sound of hammers where men and women hastily boarded up windows and doors. Vonvalt looked to the abbey, to see its windows aglow with hearthlight.

Both men started as a great peal of thunder boomed above. Lightning flickered and flashed, backlighting the clouds. Vonvalt fancied he saw faces in that black mass, screaming spectral visages. Below, the ocean crashed into the black cliffs. The harbour was now completely overwhelmed, and it was hard to think of this place as a once bustling trading town if these were the sorts of storms they could expect.

Except, they weren't, were they? This was not a natural storm. This was—

"The Scour."

"What's that?" Bressinger asked.

Vonvalt shook his head. "Nothing. Come; we'd better go back inside, before we are blown off this thing."

✦

IN THE END they set up in the keep, since that was where Bressinger had been first contacted. Vonvalt sat on the cold floorboards in a meditative state, whilst the storm smashed Gdansburg like an enormous mallet.

"I can hear screaming," Bressinger said quietly. "On the wind. Can you hear that?"

"Yes. Quiet. Let me concentrate."

The wind continued to moan and sing and scream through the castle's many apertures. The rain began in earnest, too, filling the place with the constant drip and trickle of water. It pattered down in miniature waterfalls from where tiles had dislodged and wooden beams had decayed. Vonvalt began to doubt his faith in the sturdiness of the old structure. Given enough time, wind and rain, scouring brine, and the relentless thrashing from the Meridian, and this place would succumb.

He sat there for what felt like a very long time, waiting, breathing deeply, concentrating. Bressinger, on the other hand, was a coiled spring, pacing the room ceaselessly. Vonvalt knew there was nothing he could say or do to make the man sit still and be quiet; besides, he was simply pleased to have some company. Vonvalt's courage was beyond question, but that did not mean he *enjoyed* these supernatural intrigues.

It was some time around the tenth bell when it began.

"Is that you, or is it our guest?" Vonvalt asked.

"It's not me," Bressinger said, who had, for the first time in a long time, managed to keep still and silent.

Vonvalt strained to hear over the raging of the storm. He looked about the hall, though the constant flashing lightning kept fouling his night vision.

"If you can hear me," Vonvalt said in a steady voice, "I am here in the spirit of peace and friendship."

He turned as someone whispered in his ear. He looked back over to where Bressinger stood, but the man was concealed in shadow, and as silent as the grave.

Around and above him, the old timbers creaked.

"If there is something you want to say to me, or show me, now is the time," Vonvalt said.

His skin roughed into pale gooseflesh as once again there came an unintelligible whisper in his ear. Suddenly the temperature in the hall dropped, and Vonvalt saw his breath streaming away from his mouth in a great flurry of vapour.

Now he stood, and looked around.

"Look to the Scour," Bressinger said from behind him. Vonvalt turned.

"Is she there? Is she talking to you?"

He squinted. There was something wrong with Bressinger's eyes. They were reflective, like a cat's.

Vonvalt stepped back, hand going to his sword.

"Down," Bressinger said, entranced. "We must… go down."

"Dubine, is that you?"

Silence. Stillness and silence.

"Dubine?"

DOWN! shrieked a discorporate voice, and Vonvalt cried out. He approached Bressinger quickly, but the man was catatonic. Vonvalt felt for his pulse, to find that he was still alive, his heart still beating, still drawing breath into his lungs. But it was clear from the way he stood that he was not going to say or do anything for some time.

"Fuck," Vonvalt muttered. He looked around, and then made for a doorway to the south. Here he came out into a small side chamber, a place that might once have been a private chapel, though he couldn't be certain. At the end was a barred hole through which cold salt air thundered upwards. Vonvalt looked through it, though it was too small for him to fit through, and in any event was positioned directly above a hundred-foot drop into the ocean.

He continued to explore the old chapel—for it was a chapel, he saw that now—until he found an old spiral staircase concealed behind an altar that had been stacked up in the corner. There was no torch to be lit, nor a candle, and he descended into the depths of the keep like a lump of food down a gullet.

Eventually he came into the undercroft, which smelt strongly of damp. Here he could see nothing at all, although the vault was intermittently lit by lightning filtering through the vent in the centre of the chamber. He approached it. The grille had rusted through completely, and as he peered down, he saw what looked like an old and treacherous coastal path cut into the side of the siltstone. The thing couldn't have been more than two feet across, and was about fifty feet up the side of the cliff face. Beneath, the ocean roiled like a mass of furious black snakes.

"Prince of Hell," he muttered, peering into the gloom. Water, both rain and brine, lashed the rock with such violence that it sprayed upwards through the hole. "There's no way—" he muttered to himself, and then there was a great thumping clatter above. He felt his way back to the spiral staircase and ascended, to find that the trapdoor had closed. Try as he might, he could not shift it at all.

He moved back into the undercroft and felt around, but there was nothing in that vault except the profoundly uninviting vent.

He shed his cloak, and then stood there for a little while.

"You want me to go through?" he asked, feeling foolish and frightened. Something in the air shifted. It was already too dark for it to darken still, but it was overcome by a *thickness*, a tangible sense of frustration and longing. It was like the undercroft had been clear, and was now full of greasy smoke, except the smoke was human feeling made manifest.

Vonvalt stood in the centre of this rancid cocktail of unspent hate, trying to see and feel past what his body was telling him—which was to scream and run away as fast as he could. At the core of this malaise was a deep vexation, a sense of trying to pass on a message.

Or a warning.

With gritted teeth, he climbed over the side of the vent, which was formed of a mortared stone circle in the centre of the undercroft, and, avoiding the rusted prongs of the former grille, lowered himself on to the siltstone. He almost lost his footing immediately, thanks to an incredible blast of frigid air which threatened to carry him into the rocky depths below.

"Nema damn this madness!" he shouted, though he might as well have whispered over the calamitous noise of the storm. Above, he could see the keep and lighthouse looming, the pyracantha thrashing in the wind, the whole place looking about five minutes from being erased altogether. Matria Klement had not been exaggerating. This was an unnaturally violent storm.

Gripping the wet rock as tightly as his fingers would permit, he shuffled with minuscule increments to the south, pressing himself into the siltstone with as much of his body as possible. He had done many foolhardy things in the service of the Emperor, but this had to have been the most insane. The malicious designs of men, the would-be murderer, the enemy soldier—hell, even the vast, incomprehensible insanity of the holy dimensions—he could grapple and contend with. But there was nothing to be done in the face of such raw, natural power. He might as well have been an ant.

Time passed slowly. The path was ill-defined, and would have been a difficult feat on a dry, sunny day. Minute by minute, hour by hour, he inched across, consistently astonished by how close the castle remained in spite of his labours. By the time he reached the lowest part of the headland, it had gone midnight, and the storm showed no sign of abating.

Soaking and freezing, he staggered off the cliff face and followed the path where it broadened out and followed the contour of the coastline. After quarter of an hour, he was at sea level, and in and amongst the enormous saltmarsh which stretched for several miles south of Gdansburg. Here, as Klement had alluded to, the violence of the storm had driven enormous questing channels of brine into the marsh and gouged it down to the peat. Huge turbid fingers of saltwater flowed back into the Meridian with incredible force, as Vonvalt quickly found when he accidentally stepped into one. In seconds he was being dragged out to sea, and it was only thanks to a tenacious tuft of thick, woody purslane that he prevented himself from being drowned. Using it as an anchor, he clawed his way back out of the marsh and on to the relatively solid ground abutting it. There he lay, sucking in deep, rain-soaked lungsful of breath, caked head to toe in black peat.

He stared up at the storm, trying to make sense of what he had just done and witnessed. He was certain he had been compelled by some non-earthly force. In the same way Bressinger seemed to have been lulled into some arcane catatonia, so Vonvalt seemed to have been compelled to undertake a suicidal course of action that in normal circumstances he wouldn't have dreamt of.

Eventually he dragged himself to his feet and pulled himself along the fresh channel in the saltmarsh, clambering through the mud and peat, finding purchase wherever he could. A little way ahead he saw a branch sticking out of the marsh bed, a perfect handhold to get himself out of this place and find a hot bath.

His muscles were burning and his breath laboured in his chest as he crawled towards it and gripped it by its thickest part.

And then he stopped.

He looked down, waiting for the lightning's illumination.

Too soft for a branch. Even after all these years.

There was a flash, and a great peal of thunder, as though someone had detonated a hundred barrels of blackpowder all at once.

No, not a branch.

A hand. An arm.

A corpse.

VIII
MIND DIVIDED

"Virtuous behaviour is a reward in itself. A person does not receive—nor should they expect—praise, profit, or any other honour for not committing a criminal offence."

—From Caterhauser's *The Sovan Criminal Code: Advice to Practitioners*

BLOODY NEMA!" AUGUST swore as Vonvalt barged into her chamber in the Brass Wyvern. She took a moment to look him up and down, blinking in the wan candlelight. "What *happened*? You look like you've just crawled out of a cesspit."

"I need your help," he said, breathing heavily, wild-eyed.

"Konrad," August said, standing and reaching for her heavy brown leather duster. "What's going on?"

"Quickly, Resi. I'll explain on the way. And bring your restoratives."

He returned to the street, which had been transformed into a fast-flowing river of mud. The storm was abating, though Gdansburg was still being scoured by cold, fresh winds. The very first glimmers of watery grey light were welling up on the horizon.

"There is something at work here," Vonvalt said as they hurried through the streets. There was neither hair nor hide of any of the townsfolk, who hid behind locked, bolted, and boarded doors and windows, and either slept or cowered and prayed.

August swore as she nearly tripped over a great mass of sticks deposited by the storm in the centre of the road. Everything was coated in mud, and all the thoroughfares were littered with debris.

"Where is Dubine?"

"That's the first thing I need help with."

He led her into the castle, and to where Bressinger stood—or rather, had finally slumped.

"Something took him, took hold of him," Vonvalt said as they both squatted down next to him.

"You mean he was possessed?"

"I believe so. But ineffectively. The spirit here is weak, the connexion to the mortal plane tenuous. We are just getting echoes of her rage, and the same message over and over again."

"Look to the Scour."

"Right."

They carefully laid out Bressinger on the floor, and August fished around in her satchel. Vonvalt heard the clink of glass, and she withdrew a restorative and unstoppered it. Then, carefully, she tipped it into Bressinger's mouth.

"Fucking hell!" he spluttered as he bolted upright, coughing and hacking and retching. Then he spent several long moments spitting repeatedly on the floor. "Nema and Savare and all the saints! What the fuck was that?"

Vonvalt gripped him by the shoulders. "Are you all right?"

"No!" Bressinger spat. "I feel like I've just drunk one-hundred-proof shit."

"Do you remember anything?" Vonvalt pressed.

"About what? Where the hell am I?"

"Gdansburg," August said patiently. "In the lighthouse keep."

Bressinger pressed a hand to his head, wincing. "The bloody haunted lighthouse. Yes." He looked around. "Yes, I remember. What happened to me? Did someone knock me out?"

"In a manner of speaking," Vonvalt said, standing up. "There's more to do. I can explain everything later, but we must move quickly."

"Wait a minute!" Bressinger called out, kneading his skull with his fists, but Vonvalt and August were already hurrying back outside.

✦

THE ARM WAS still there. Vonvalt had taken some time to mark its location with as many sticks as he could find, but with the storm, and the great gouges driven into the saltmarsh, the risk was that it was all swept away by the retreating channels of seawater.

"Good gods," August said as the three of them stood on the firm ground nearby.

"Indeed," Vonvalt said. He was exhausted, and wanted nothing more than to have a hot bath and a good long sleep. Instead, a very, *very* long day awaited.

"Let's get on with it then," Bressinger said, taking a step forward.

"Wait!" Vonvalt shouted—too late. His taskman sank up to his waist in the marsh.

"Bloody hell!" Bressinger growled, struggling ineffectually against the thick, soupy peat.

"Idiot!" Vonvalt thundered. He bent forward, and gripped Bressinger under the armpits, but try as he might, and even with August's help, he could not get the man free. "You'll just have to live there," he snapped.

"Get me out of this fucking bog!" Bressinger shouted, beginning to panic. "I'm sinking!"

"I'll get some help," August muttered, and ran back towards the town.

"Get a horse!" Vonvalt called after her. He crouched down on the saltgrass. "I'm just going to sit here awhile," he muttered to Bressinger. "Resi will be back in a minute."

"Please don't let me drown in this mud."

"Don't be so dramatic."

✦

IT WAS DAWN by the time they got a rope under Bressinger's arms. He had sunk up to his neck in the peat, and was beginning to panic in a manner quite unlike him.

Ten yards away, a gaggle of Gdansburgers hitched the other end of the rope to a shirehorse.

"Slowly!" Vonvalt called.

"Quickly!" Bressinger shouted.

"Shut up! Do you want to be pulled in half?"

"…No."

They spent ten minutes carefully, slowly, easing Bressinger out of the sucking marsh. He lay on the saltgrass like fresh foxshit. "Sweet Nema, Blessed Nema."

"We'll need to construct some sort of pontoon," Vonvalt said to the horse's owner, ignoring his taskman. "Nice and broad."

"Probably want some barrels for buoyancy, too," the woman said.

"Yes. Good," Vonvalt replied. "There should be plenty of spare wood going after that storm. Can I trust you to pull together a work party?"

The woman nodded, eyes not leaving the withered—but otherwise well preserved—arm sticking out of the peat. "Who is she?"

Vonvalt shrugged. "I've no idea. But I can assure you, madam, I am going to find out."

⸻✦⸻

WORK BEGAN ON the platform. Vonvalt walked down to the ocean, and, to the amusement of the townsfolk, stripped off and bathed in the frigid brine, washing away all of the dried black peat that covered him in a cracked crust. Then he stood waist-deep in the water, looking out to the horizon.

"What are you thinking about?" August called out from behind him.

"Nothing."

"I don't believe that for a moment. I don't think you ever stop thinking. It is your blessing and curse."

He smiled sadly. "Perhaps. Did you find Havener, by the way?"

"With the marsh harrier. He is being held in an inn about five miles north of here."

"Well done."

"I brought you some fresh clothes."

"Thank you."

"I think it will be a few hours until we are ready to pull up the body. Why don't you rest?"

"Honestly, Resi?" he turned back to the ocean. "I'm afraid of what I might dream about."

⸻✦⸻

IN FACT IT wasn't until noon that the townsfolk had constructed a platform stable enough to attempt the recovery of the body. By that time, Klement had arrived, conspicuously alone. She was wearing a large white overcloak which bore the black star of Saint Saxanhilde.

"You were a templar?" Vonvalt asked her.

"In another life," she replied brusquely. She nodded her chin at the revealed arm. "Do you have any idea who it is?"

"Madam, I was about to ask you the same question."

Klement shook her head, sticking out her bottom lip. "Could be anybody. That's black peat; the corpse could be a thousand years old."

Vonvalt looked at her pointedly. "I suspect not, given the *goings on* in the lighthouse."

"Aye, perhaps not," she said quietly.

"Anyone reported missing or killed that you can call to mind?"

"Gdansburg has been slowly emptying of folk for two years," Klement said bitterly. "It could be anyone. Or it could be the body of someone merely passing through. This road used to be very well trafficked." She shrugged. "Might not even be a murder. You saw how your man nearly went in. The marsh is treacherous. It could claim anyone who wasn't paying attention."

"We will be able to tell easily enough if she drowned," Vonvalt said.

"How?"

"Her lungs will be full of water."

"You intend to cut her open?"

"If I must."

Klement shook her head. "I don't think I can permit such desecration."

"'Tis not desecration. It is the forensic method. And besides," he added sternly. "It is not within your gift to prevent me."

He expected her to give him another dose of her sharp tongue, but she simply nodded. "I won't fight you any more, Justice."

"I know what you think of me, and the Empire, Matria, but I really am trying to help you."

"If you say so," she muttered, and went to speak to the labourers.

THEY HAD A little lunch, and then Vonvalt climbed on to the platform and squatted down over the body. "She's well preserved, but I don't want to pull her to pieces during the extraction."

"We'll have to tie ropes around her midriff, arms, and legs," Bressinger said.

Vonvalt nodded. "Get to it, then. Has the physician been notified?"

"She has. She's waiting to receive the body," one of the townsfolk called.

They passed ropes underneath the body, with several people sinking up to their shoulders in the peat to secure them. The process was difficult and painstaking, and thanks to Vonvalt's constant interruption and direction, took half an hour. Eventually they had secured, to the best of their ability, three ropes under the corpse, and once again used the shirehorse to slowly lever her free.

There went up a great groan of dismay as the body came out of the marsh. She was completely intact, though fully caked in black peat. They carried her gently and reverently to an old sail which someone had brought up from the harbour, and wrapped her in it. Then they placed her in a cart, and hitched the cart to the shirehorse.

Vonvalt looked over to Klement, who was weeping quietly, and saying a prayer.

"Come on," Vonvalt muttered to August and Bressinger. "We have work to do."

✦

THE PHYSICIAN WAS a surprisingly young woman, red-haired like many of the settled Brigalanders, and had a large moth tattoo over her throat. She wore a simple blue kirtle and a blouse with the sleeves rolled up to her elbows.

"Hullo," Bressinger said awkwardly as they entered the mortuary.

"Mister Bressinger," she said with perfect professionalism

"I am Justice Sir Konrad Vonvalt," he said, "and this is Justice Lady Resi August."

"Gerda Laursen," the physician replied. They both went to clasp her forearm in the traditional Sovan greeting, which she clearly had not expected, and there were several moments of awkward hand and arm touching, welcomely foreclosed by two men bringing the body in.

"Just here, please," the physician said, and the men laid it on the floor in the corner, before leaving.

"You do not want it on the bench?" Vonvalt asked.

"I was told we would be washing it?" Laursen said, pointing to a drain in the floor and several buckets of water which stood in a line next to the wall.

"Ah, indeed."

They peeled back the sailcloth, and then Laursen began the unenviable task of cleaning the body. They watched this macabre spectacle with a mixture of fascination and unease.

"Have you been in Gdansburg for long?" Vonvalt asked her.

"Actually no," she replied. "I came here to take orders in the kloster, but I found it did not suit me."

"How long ago was that?"

"Three—no, four... and a half years. Nema, where does the time go?"

She soaked a cloth in the bucket of water and gently washed away the peat. It took Vonvalt a little while to realise that the woman's skin had been dyed near black during the strange, natural mummification process, and had a slightly glossy, leathery quality, like the carapace of a beetle.

"Do you have any idea who this is?" Vonvalt asked.

Laursen took a moment to examine the woman's face, running a hand tenderly down her cheek. "No," she said sadly.

"Matria Klement seems to think it could be just about anybody."

"I daresay she's right. A lot of people used to transition through this part of the world."

She continued to wash the peat away, and the drain gurgled with the iron-smelling black water. When the process was done, and

Laursen had covered the corpse's modesty with another rag, Vonvalt squatted down.

"May I?" he asked.

"By all means."

Vonvalt laid a hand on the woman's breastbone. His brow furrowed. He palpated the chest, and then the ribs, and then the body's bony protuberances more generally.

"What is it?" August asked.

"It's remarkable," Vonvalt said, withdrawing his hand. "The skin and hair are almost perfectly preserved, but the bones are soft as clay."

"As though she has been beaten?"

Vonvalt shook his head. "No one could be beaten this thoroughly without the skin telling the tale. 'Tis as though she has been crushed under an enormous rock, though there is no sign of it anywhere."

"Must be some natural process," August said.

"Aye," Laursen agreed. "These soils have a unique quality, like vinegar. I've used peat in many counter-pox remedies."

"You think the soil has dissolved her bones?"

Laursen shrugged. "It's possible."

"But not her skin?"

"I'm just theorising."

Vonvalt clacked his tongue. He gently rolled the body on to one side, examining her back.

"How old would you say this woman is?" he asked August.

"I'd stake a year's wages she's not a day over twenty."

"Younger still," Vonvalt agreed. "Seventeen, eighteen perhaps." He worked his way up to the head, and examined the scalp, gently parting the hair and looking for any sign of a blow to the head.

"Anything?" August asked.

"No. Take a look yourself."

August did, and concurred with Vonvalt's assessment.

"Will you...?" Vonvalt asked her, and she nodded. "Dubine, come."

He left with Bressinger and waited outside the door for a couple of minutes, until August called him back in.

"Anything?"

August shrugged. "Honestly, with the state of the body, impossible to tell."

"No contusions?"

"Not that I can see."

"All right." Vonvalt turned to Laursen. "I'd like to see her lungs."

The physician paused. "Her lungs?"

Vonvalt nodded. "I want to see if she drowned."

"You want me to cut her open and pull out her lungs?"

"Well, just one of them." When the woman gave him a look of disgust, he added, "Madam, most physicians I know have to be physically restrained from cutting up dead bodies. People make it their entire business to dig up corpses and sell them to barbers in Sova."

"Do you not think this poor girl has been through enough?"

"I am certain this young lady has endured an experience more terrible than any of us can imagine. But she is long dead, and this body is just decaying matter. The most just thing to do now would be to find out what happened to her, and bring her killer to account."

"If she was killed," Bressinger said.

"Murdered, you mean. Obviously she has been killed."

"Why must you sic your pedanticness on us all the time?"

"Pedantry."

"Git," Bressinger muttered.

"Madam Laursen; please. The body's lungs are coming out one way or the other. And I am certain you will do it with much more skill and reverence than I."

Laursen sighed. "Fine," she said. "But I would like a prayer said for her first."

"I'll fetch a nun," Bressinger sighed, and left.

✦

IT WAS LATE in the afternoon by the time the three of them reconvened in the Brass Wyvern. The place had been flooded, and the common room was coated in a layer of silt which the owner, prostitutes, and even some of the longtime regulars were at pains to scrub out.

They went upstairs to Vonvalt's chamber with a flagon of wine and three pewter goblets, and sat drinking and smoking in silence.

"Drowned," Vonvalt said. "The only question remaining is whether it was done deliberately or not."

"Do you think the body is what Osgar Erikson saw in the marsh? The sheriff's ledger specifically referenced the lad having seen something there," Bressinger said.

"Or perhaps the ghost of the woman who had once inhabited it," August murmured.

"Seeing a corpse might render a young boy insensible with fear," Vonvalt said. "But she would have been submerged in the peat."

"*You* saw her."

"I saw her because her arm had been left exposed by the storm. Otherwise I would never have seen her. No one could have." He thought a little more, looking out the window to where the townsfolk moved through the streets, clearing the debris left in the wake of—even by these curious, arcane standards—an unnaturally violent storm. "Something happened here two years ago. Something unpleasant. And I fear that everyone who might have given us answers is dead."

"Except Havener," Bressinger said.

"Aye. And in ordinary circumstances, I would use the Emperor's Voice on him and turn his mind inside out like a sack full of potatoes. But I can't."

He smoked his pipe in silence for a long minute.

"Don't," August said, refilling her goblet.

"I'm considering it."

"Do not!"

"Do not what?" Bressinger asked.

August ignored him. "It will destroy you. It's madness. There'll be nothing left in there except total insanity."

"The body was remarkably well preserved."

"Konrad: she died at least two years ago."

"Aye, but she is still *here*!" Vonvalt snapped. He brandished his hand in the direction of the lighthouse. "Do you not see? The peat has preserved her, body and soul. Her spirit cannot move on. It is locked in this… *liminal* place. And in unearthing her, we have set the clock running. We have a very limited window."

Now Bressinger's expression changed from confusion to horror. "You do not mean to perform a séance with that bog body, do you?"

"That is precisely what I mean to do. And I am going to have to do it tonight."

"Nema, *why*?"

"Because we have taken it out of its preservative fluid. Exposed it to air. Surely it will wither and decay, now."

"Who are you asking? Because I can assure you, neither I nor Dubine know the answer." August leant forward, giving Vonvalt an imploring look. "What I do know is this: performing any sort of necromantic rite on such an old corpse is an invitation to suicide. It is one of the first things they teach you in the Magistratum. Her spirit, whatever once tethered her to this mortal plane, will have been chum for demons and interdimensional predators for *years*, Konrad. And you propose to jump into the midst of it."

"The danger was always overstated," Vonvalt lied.

"I will not help you do this."

"I do not need your help."

"Do not be foolish! You will need one of us to act as the beacon for the Nyrsanar Nexi."

"Dubine will do it."

"The fuck I will!" Bressinger grunted.

"She's exaggerating!" Vonvalt said. "This might be our last chance to find out what happened here."

"It is one thing to risk your own life—to say nothing of your immortal soul. But don't drag Dubine into it."

"I'm not going to drag anybody into anything," Vonvalt said irritably. "I'm perfectly capable of performing the rite myself."

"You will get lost down there."

"So be my beacon!"

August made a frustrated noise. "How can you be so obstinate?"

"I think it's what makes me a good Justice," Vonvalt said with jarring sincerity. Then he drained the last of his wine. "I'm not going to do anything right now. I need to get a couple of hours' sleep. But we should have the body moved back to the lighthouse. The spirit energy is strongest there. And I shall perform the séance at the third bell."

August rolled her eyes.

"Dubine; could you go and fetch Havener please. Resi will tell you where he is being held."

"It's a ten mile round trip," August said.

"Then we shall see him on the morrow, won't we!" Vonvalt snapped. "Blood of gods, out, the pair of you, and do something useful!"

IX
ECHOES OF MEMORY

"The mob of commonfolk who will form a posse, and take a killer, and cut his head off down by the river, is the same mob who will form a jury, and presented with the same evidence, will choose to imprison—or even acquit. The difference is process. The good lawkeeper knows that effective process must be a dispassionate affair, severe and serious, and beggared of all the choler that made the commission of the crime possible in the first place."

—From Caterhauser's *The Sovan Criminal Code: Advice to Practitioners*

THE TOWNSFOLK WOULD not help take the body into the lighthouse, and so Vonvalt had to do it by himself. He waited until after dark, and then he and Laursen moved through Gdansburg like grave robbers. The body was very light. There was something melancholy about that.

"I will lay you to rest," Vonvalt promised quietly in a rare indulgence of sentimentality. "I swear it."

As they approached the threshold of the castle courtyard, even the physician paused.

"For Nema's sake," Vonvalt muttered, and holding the bog body like he had just rescued someone from a burning building, walked into the keep.

Above, thunder rumbled.

He waited then again, meditating. He regretted his sharp words to August and Bressinger. He took their friendship—to say nothing of their brains and brawn—totally for granted. August was right; Sova was changing him, and not for the better. Vonvalt was not a man given to making apologies often, but there were also not many people whom he valued more than being correct.

The rain began again, though the storm did not achieve anything like the violence of the night before. He sat next to the body, eyes closed, hands on his knees, preparing himself for the rite. He had next to him the *Grimoire Necromantia*, one of the oldest and most restricted books the Magistratum had produced. It was a manual on how to access the afterlife, a highly unpredictable process in which a Justice used a—normally fresh—dead body to descend into the holy dimensions. Necromancy was the most powerful tool in a Justice's arsenal, but it was a talent few could grasp. Vonvalt was a rarity in that not only could he do it, but he was good at it.

The second bell had just tolled when he heard footsteps. His heart lurched, and he was prepared to be confronted by an angry spirit again, when he looked up and saw August walking through the keep.

"Thank you," he said quietly. "For coming."

"And?"

"I am sorry. For being such an arse."

August nodded once. "I accept." She looked at the body, and then Vonvalt. "Where do you want me?"

Vonvalt turned to the small bag of effects he had brought with him, and withdrew a silver deer's head medallion. "Put this on," he said, and she did. "You remember what to do?"

"Do I remember the words to speak?"

"Yes."

She thought a moment. "Yes."

"It's important."

"I remember them, Konrad."

"All right."

They both looked at the body. "What do you think happened here?" she asked Vonvalt.

"I'm hoping this will give me the answer."

"Don't get lost down there, Konrad."

"Believe me, I have no desire to."

Above them the storm worsened. August studied the decaying beams of the old keep.

"You are cutting to the heart of something," she murmured.

"I think so," he replied. "Now; peace. Let me prepare."

✦

HE BEGAN AT the third bell, a time of significance in the Neman orthodoxy. With the body arranged correctly, and a candle lit, Vonvalt opened the grimoire.

"After the words, you must not touch me," he said.

"I remember," August said, holding the medallion. Then she and Vonvalt faced one another, and August put her hand on Vonvalt's shoulder, and they spoke in High Saxan, "*Azshtre stovakato bratnya to zi chovekna eyrsvet linata. Kogata govoria dumitenta boga maĭka, toĭmoz daesevŭrne vyr zemyatra nazivite.*"

The candle flickered. The keep darkened. August took several steps back. Then Vonvalt positioned himself at the body's feet, and spoke a second time—the Nyrsanar Navi, the descendant incantation.

As he did so, the world faded around him.

⸻◆⸻

HE AWOKE TO find himself in another type of marsh. Not the saltmarsh of Gdansburg, though it was strikingly reminiscent. This was the Plain of Burden, the *Edaximae*, the Purgatorial dimension. It was an infinite plane, one of murky grey water, dead blackened trees, a roiling grey sky, and most striking of all, the bottom of what looked like an enormous astral funnel, a huge black cone swirling with stars and colourful streamers of cloud. This was a place of absolute stillness and silence, a place where sound seemed like a foreign concept. The air did not move; there was no wind. He did not even breathe. There was no need. Here, he—or rather, his spiritual avatar—was not alive in any meaningful sense.

He began to wade through the water. This was not a place of logic or reason. It was a place of feeling, and intuition, a place that defied comprehension and which faded from memory at the earliest opportunity. It was a place the mind rejected as foreign, forbidden; a place impermissible to know and totally against the natural order of things.

He walked on for a little while until he was certain something was following him. It was not that he could hear a second pair of legs wading through the death-soaked muck around him; it was some nameless prey instinct. He turned; in the faraway distance was a cloaked figure, draped in the body of a dead sheep. The figure pointed to him, a silent threat.

A promise.

"Shit," Vonvalt said, ready to abandon the séance entirely; but then the plane was shifting. The ground beneath his feet, hardly solid to begin with, was sinking. Not just where he stood, but all around him. A vast tract of it, sliding downwards like a landslip.

His heart lurched as he dropped. He fell through a vast hole, falling, falling, all around him waterfalls of grey slime, until—

✦

HE WAS IN a forest, but not one of trees. Here, hundreds of dead black arms jutted up from the ground, whilst a cold, powerful wind scoured the bleak landscape.

Scoured.

There was a voice on the wind, a distant scream, constant whispers. In the very corners of his vision, dark shapes danced and flickered, and disappeared the moment he turned.

The scream came again. It was not a woman. It was a little boy.

What was his name?

Osgar Erikson.

He said the name out loud. And everything shifted again.

✦

DARKNESS. HE COULD hear a voice. It was a familiar voice—Bronislav Havener. He was talking in hushed, angry tones. Vonvalt could hear a girl's voice, too. She sounded frightened.

He advanced through the darkness, willing for it to part. He couldn't *see* anything. Just a great thick blackness, an oleaginous cloud of malaise, of ill feeling, of fear and hatred.

He could smell brine. Hear gulls.

Suddenly the blackness cleared. He was back in Gdansburg, or rather, a washed out simulacrum of it. He was not himself. He was Erikson. He was catching marsh frogs. He caught them and took them home and showed his parents. He loved his parents. Vonvalt felt the love fill him as he thought of Freya and Erik. An innocent, dependent love. They were kind parents, and he a good boy.

There was a second feeling, too. Unease. He was a little far from home, and there were lots of strangers who moved through the town to the north and east. There had been an incident recently with Dennish deserters, men fleeing the Sovan Legions. Osgar didn't really understand. Vonvalt's own understanding imposed itself in the boy's mind—in the *echo* of the boy's mind. The boy was dead, and this was a memory of a memory, imprinted on the aether, as ephemeral as an eyeblink.

The boy caught the marsh frog in a little net his father had made and gave out a delighted squeal. He was not too frightened; there were people nearby. A man and a woman. He was not afraid of women. Women didn't hurt children, not really. Vonvalt's interloping mind knew this was not the case, but Osgar was not six years old, and had no concept of the capriciousness of the world.

He had nearly turned and gone home. That was the tragedy, or part of it. Vonvalt—in spite of everything, in spite of how iron hard his soul had become to these dismal goings-on, these wretched crimes, the brutality and callousness of human men and women, in spite of how much horror he had seen and dealt with and tried and punished—still willed the boy to run. He willed it with every fibre of the part of him that existed in this place. *Run, lad! Run! Run as fast as your little legs will take you! Get help! Find adults to help you! Find good people! They do exist, I swear it!*

But the story was two years played out, and there was nothing he could do.

I swear there are good people, Vonvalt said, but here was one bad one—an evil one, in fact—and there was nothing he nor the boy could do.

The boy watched the man drown the woman, first with confusion, then with a level of fear that bordered on mania. Even as the deed was done, and the man thrust the woman deep into the peat under the saltmarsh, and advanced on the boy, the boy did not move. He was stuck fast, as though his feet had sprouted roots and anchored him to his death.

YOU WILL SPEAK OF THIS TO NO ONE, Havener said in the Emperor's Voice. It could be tempered, the Voice. It was the one power common to all Justices. Those who could not master it were turned out of the Magistratum. Used to its full effect, it could stop hearts dead in chests, or—as in this case—vacate a brain of its conscious mind, like someone whisking away a tablecloth.

Havener had hit Erikson with such a psychic blast that even in this broken, aethereal memory, Vonvalt winced with the force of it. He felt the boy's thoughts dissolve, to be replaced by little more than base impulses and a singular fixation on the saltmarsh and the horror it now represented. It seemed Havener, as ghastly as he was, was content to divorce the boy of his mind rather than kill him outright, for after a brief, rough examination, he swept on, and through the town, and away to the east.

Vonvalt puppeteered the boy's body over to where the young woman had been plunged into the marsh. There should have been nothing to see—just some broken weeds and turbid water. But instead he saw the girl floating over an enormous bank of cloud, as though she had been laid flat on a plate of glass, whilst beneath her a violent tempest raged.

Then the girl lunged upwards, and grabbed him by the arm. "Look to the Scour!" she pleaded, and then the invisible barrier was broken, and Vonvalt was swept into the storm and tossed around like a ragdoll.

The last thing he saw was a shining white deer somewhere high above, before all was black oblivion.

X
THE RIPPLE EFFECT

"Like a good legal textbook, one must be wary of the spirit dimensions. It is easy to get lost down there."

—From Caterhauser's *The Sovan Criminal Code: Advice to Practitioners*

"KONRAD? KONRAD? FOR Nema's sake, speak to me you bloody fool!"

"I'm here," he said quietly, tiredly. "I'm here."

"Did it work?"

He opened his eyes slowly. He was lying on the floor, next to the body. Nothing had moved, except apparently him. The silver medallion around August's neck was lightly smoking.

"Yes."

She helped him up. "You were weeping."

"Weeping?"

"Aye. I have never seen you look so anguished."

Vonvalt touched around his eyes, to find his cheeks were indeed wet with tears.

"It was unpleasant."

"What did you see?"

Vonvalt told her. August listened in silence, and then sat in silence for a long time after he had finished.

"Were people always capable of such wickedness?" she said eventually.

"Since the dawn of time. But Justices… Justices should not be capable of it."

August looked at him, her head cocked to one side. "You truly believe that, don't you?"

"I have to," he replied, and stood.

"Why?"

"Because otherwise, what was it all for?"

THEY WENT BACK into Gdansburg, and returned the body to Laursen, though she had gone to bed, and had to be roused. Then they went to Klement, and roused her too, and Vonvalt told her what had happened. She seemed to be exceptionally displeased to learn of the séance, as most Nemans tended to be when reminded of the powers that had once belonged to the Church.

"So what you are telling me, Justice, is that Havener is not only guilty of murdering Osgar Erikson, but of someone else entirely?"

"Yes. Do you have any notion of who the girl is? Was anybody reported killed or missing at the time Erikson lost his wits?"

"If somebody had been reported killed at the same time, do you not think we would have brought it to your attention?"

"I don't think you would have done any such thing," Vonvalt snapped. "Madam, you have come within a hairsbreadth of being arrested yourself."

"Well we are past that now," she said.

"You had better hope so."

Klement thought a moment. "People were constantly coming and going through Gdansburg then. And then, after the…" She drifted off. "So you're telling me that it is the spirit of this young woman that has been haunting the lighthouse?"

"Yes."

"And the Scour was—"

"An eldritch storm. She was trying to uncover her own body."

Klement digested this. "We are cursed."

"Matria; was there anybody missing from the town at that time?"

"The only person I can think of is… Lissi Vang," Klement said. Something happened to her expression then. There was a flash of something—to Vonvalt it looked like panic—followed by a period of silent, frenzied thought. "But she wasn't killed," she added, an undercurrent of disbelief in her voice. She shook her head. "No. She ran away. Eloped. With a Dennish deserter."

Vonvalt exchanged a look with August. "You know this?"

Klement looked as though she was going to be sick. "It was reported to the sheriff. He sent men looking for her."

"Did they find her?"

"Well…" Klement said, shifting in her seat. Then her features twisted into anger. "Are you telling me that one of your Justices murdered our Lissi?"

"I'm telling you that I am *accusing* him of murder—"

"Don't you use your lawman's word tricks on me!"

"Do not shout at me—"

"That man needs to be put down like a dog!"

"Madam, if he is guilty of these crimes, then he will be killed, there's no question of that."

"I don't believe you. You're going to take him back to Sova. I know it. I feel it in my bones. All you Justices, all you Sovans, all you Imperials are exactly the same."

"Matria—"

"Get out! Get out of my abbey and never come back!" she screamed, and they left.

"OUR FIRST PRIORITY must be to protect Sir Bronislav," Vonvalt said as they approached the brothel. "The townsfolk will seek to lynch him."

"And what is it that you will seek to do?" August asked.

"I shall have to try him."

"You have enough to put him to the sword."

Vonvalt shook his head. "There is no precedent for a Justice executing another Justice. Besides," he said, as they reached the entrance. "I think it would be a good thing for the people of Gdansburg to see some due process."

They entered, and Vonvalt summoned the barkeep. The man was still clad in his nightclothes when he came downstairs.

"Breakfast, was it?" he asked wearily.

"Lissi Vang. I'm looking for her parents, or if not her parents then whoever looked after her here."

The barkeep thought a moment. "Well, old Silas Vang kicked it last year. But her ma is still about, Mette."

"Could you show me where she lives?"

"...Right now?"

"Right now."

"All right. Let me get my clothes on."

"ALF?" A GREY-HAIRED woman asked as she answered the door to her longhouse.

"Morning Mette," the barkeep said. "This is, er—"

"Justice Sir Konrad Vonvalt and Justice Lady Resi August," he said. "May we speak with you, madam?"

"Regarding what?" the woman asked warily, pulling a blanket around her.

"Your daughter," August said.

The woman's hand went to her heart, and her expression fell. "You have heard from her?" When neither Justice answered, she began trembling. "It's bad news, isn't it? I knew it. I had a dream about it last night. She appeared to me and told me goodbye."

"Will you come with me to the physician's?" Vonvalt asked Mette.

"Why? What's there?"

"We recovered the body of a young woman from the marsh yesterday—"

August darted forward as the woman collapsed, managing to stop her from cracking her head on the doorjamb.

"Fetch me a strong drink, would you?" Vonvalt asked the barkeep.

"Certainly, milord," the man said anxiously, and bustled away.

✦

A LITTLE WHILE later, when the mother had a few brandies in her and had put on some warm clothes, they made their way over to Gerda Laursen's place. The physician had been forewarned of their coming, and greeted them at the front door. The townsfolk in the street did an extremely bad job of pretending to be uninterested in what was taking place.

"How are you, Mette?" Laursen asked.

"Let's just get this over with," the woman replied.

They went down into the mortuary. This time the body had been laid on the wooden slab. Laursen had taken the time to dress the girl in a white kirtle embroidered with flowers, and had laid more wildflowers around her. It was a nice touch, but there was no ameliorating the desperate, anguished, animalistic wail that emanated from Mette Vang the moment she laid eyes on her. She threw herself across the body and screamed, and when she could no longer scream she moaned and sobbed.

Vonvalt watched these proceedings with a sad expression. Next to him, August thumbed an errant tear off her cheek. The physician cried openly, and stroked the bereaved mother's back.

"I think that answers that question," Vonvalt said quietly.

YET MORE TIME later, they were back in Mette's longhouse. There was still no sign of Bressinger, and Vonvalt asked August to once again reconnoitre the surrounding countryside with the marsh harrier to give them some forewarning of the man's arrival. It seemed that every scrap of information about this case was passed on to the town's remaining inhabitants more or less immediately, and Vonvalt was in no doubt that a large posse of men—likely the same posse that had attempted to catch Bressinger, and interdict him outside the abbey—was gathering in preparation.

"Did Lissi have anything to do with Justice Havener?" Vonvalt asked.

"You mean aside from being murdered by him?" Mette asked. There was only a trace of venom in her voice. She was as exhausted as it was possible for a human being to be, and Vonvalt knew that he would not be given long to question her.

"Aside from that. Had she, for example, gone to him with any legal complaint?"

"Not that I know of."

"Perhaps it was something that she kept from you?"

"Perhaps."

"Did she keep things from you?"

"She was a seventeen-year-old girl. She kept as much from me as she could."

"What about lovers?"

"She had lovers."

"That you knew of?"

"Yes. And doubtless some I did not."

Vonvalt thought a minute, forming case theories. "The sheriff's ledger said she eloped with a Dennish deserter. Were there any Dens here?"

"A steady stream of them at that time. Flowing down the coast like a river of shite."

Vonvalt tapped his teeth with his index fingernail. "Did you have any interaction with Justice Havener?"

"No."

"Could Lissi have?"

"You have already asked me that."

"No I mean…"

Mette looked up at him with wide, watery eyes. "Are you asking me if she had sexual relations with that man?"

"I'm asking you if you *know* of any. Not whether she did."

"I think I would like you to leave now, Justice."

Vonvalt nodded. "Thank you for your time. And I am sorry for your loss."

Outside the longhouse, there stood a large crowd of Gdansburgers.

"Return to your homes," Vonvalt said tiredly.

"Where is he?" one of them asked.

"The man is not to be touched until I have tried him."

"Did he murder Lissi Vang?" someone else called.

"These matters will all be dealt with at trial. The trial will be a public event. You are all welcome—nay, encouraged—to attend."

"This is Imperial Justice!"

"It is!" Vonvalt thundered. "By Nema, it *is* Imperial Justice! And Gdansburg is a Sovan possession, whether you like it or not! Just like it was once a Grozodan possession, before the Brigalanders sacked and settled it! And before that a Manaeii possession! And before that the birds and beasts who claimed this territory! Now it is Sovan, and there will be a Sovan trial, and judgment shall be passed, and the appropriate punishment meted out! Do you understand me?"

They might have killed him. They could easily have done it. There were thirty of them at least, and they were full of rage. Instead, they looked admonished, and cowed, and they dispersed. There was nothing quite like Vonvalt in a fury. He was like a storm.

Like the Scour.

He took no pleasure from the thought.

BRESSINGER ARRIVED IN the dead of night. Anticipating that there would be precisely the sort of confrontation Vonvalt had faced down, he had waited until the first bell, and brought Havener in on the same cart the townsfolk had used to extract him. Bound and gagged, and clad in homespun peasant clothes—and having been punched at least once in the face, judging by the bruise around his left eye socket—Havener looked more like a vagrant than anything else.

They put him in the town gaol, for his own safety, and Vonvalt decamped to the old sheriff's office above it. There he explained matters to Bressinger, whilst August took the opportunity to sleep.

"You do not think quickly having his head off is the best solution?"

"It would be the easiest thing in the world to kill him, though I am not certain I am even permitted to, on the current Magistratum rules," Vonvalt said, smoking his pipe. "Besides, there are still a few questions left unanswered."

"Such as?"

"Such as *why* he killed Ms Vang in the first place."

"I promise you the answer will be disappointing," Bressinger said. "It will not be some sweeping conspiracy involving Dens, and the Legions, and deserters. It will be the most dismally shit reason you can think of."

Vonvalt sat quietly for a moment. "I'm worried he may have murdered the sheriff, as well."

Bressinger considered this. "Fuck me. I'd forgotten about the sheriff."

"I'm also worried that the only evidence I have for Sir Bronislav having murdered her is the imprinted aethereal memory-echo of a dead five year old."

"That evidence is enough to convict anyone you care to name," Bressinger said.

"But is it enough to convict an Emperor's Justice?"

"Why should it make a difference?"

"He is an officer of the Crown. He is supposed to be utterly beyond such shabby practice. I don't think any of you appreciate the scandal this is going to cause back in Sova."

Bressinger clutched the sides of his face. "Oh heavens! Not Sova!"

Vonvalt waved him off angrily. "I am just saying, we should be prudent where we can. Besides, we have no evidence whatever that he murdered Erikson. We have *never* had any evidence—nothing except the blind insistence of the townsfolk. I am going to have to get a confession out of him."

"That man is not leaving this town alive. So do your due process if you must. Go through the motions. Let the people bathe in the holy light of the common law and Imperial Justice. And then cut his fucking head off, and let's quit this place. I am sick to my death of it."

Vonvalt watched Bressinger stalk out of the room. Then he turned to the window behind him, and looked out over the darkening town, smoking his pipe.

"As am I, Dubine. As am I."

XI
THE TRIAL

"No legal process is infallible. There will inevitably be mistakes. The innocent will be imprisoned, flogged, hanged, beheaded. Remember always, therefore, the cardinal rule: 'tis better for ten guilty men to be set free, than for one innocent man to be convicted."

—From Caterhauser's *The Sovan Criminal Code: Advice to Practitioners*

THE TOWN GAOL did have a courthouse on the north side of the building, but it was much too small. Instead, Vonvalt set up his effects in the town square.

It was a grey, blustery morning, two days after Bressinger had returned with Havener, and everyone who remained in Gdansburg had gathered to watch the proceedings. Vonvalt looked out over the sea of blonde and red hair and stony faces. Children. The elderly. The infirm. The number of people between the ages of twenty and fifty were few and far between.

There was no sign of Matria Klement.

He was on uncertain ground here. There was certainly a special ethics procedure to follow when a Justice was accused of a crime, a staid process usually involving a conclave of several Justices back in the Magistratum. Instead Vonvalt had decided to try Havener as though he were a common criminal—which, but for a procedural confection, he was.

"After all, who knows what will come out in the wash?" he murmured.

"What's that?" Bressinger asked from next to him.

Vonvalt shook his head. "Nothing."

Havener had declined any sort of representation—had answered no questions in the previous two days, and had refused to respect or participate in the proceedings at all, which inserted another splinter of doubt into Vonvalt's mind about his chosen course of action. But he had it all set up now, and it was, to him at least, a worthy enterprise. Better than simply cutting off Havener's head and chucking it in the sea.

There was no warden, and so Justice August had agreed to act as the independent adjudicator—another piece of stage management which was inappropriate given her role in the investigation, but which added another layer of procedure to these otherwise untethered proceedings. She sat behind Vonvalt's travelling desk, in front of the Sovan device which had to be weighed down thanks to the coastal wind.

"Ladies and gentlemen," Vonvalt said, addressing the jury, a selection of twenty men and women taken from the town who sat on a motley of chairs next to August. A simple majority was needed to convict, and there was not a shadow of a doubt in Vonvalt's mind that they would vote to do so. Still, it was important to have their investment in the process.

He paused, enduring one last spasm of self-doubt. Was this truly an enormous waste of time? Should he just order the man to be killed now, and leave?

"Sir Konrad?" August prompted.

He shook his head, as if to rattle the self-doubt free. "Yes. Thank you. Ladies and gentlemen, we are here today to determine the guilt of Sir Bronislav Havener. Justice Havener stands accused of the murder of Osgar Erikson and Lissi Vang."

This drew out a sudden and calamitous baying from the crowd—including from the jury—including cries of "murderer" and "guilty". Vonvalt waited a little while until it was clear that they were not going to shut up by themselves, and so he ordered them to, using a hint of the Emperor's Voice. This achieved a silence so sudden that Vonvalt wondered whether he had gone deaf.

He cleared his throat and continued through some formalities, a little procedural back-and-forth with August which once again seemed bizarre and contrived and clearly went over the heads of the people present.

And then, he laid out his case.

"On the 17th of Sorpen, 34 anno imperii Sovi, Bronislav Havener murdered Lissi Vang."

Vonvalt watched Havener's face carefully as he said it. And even though the man was a Justice of some thirty years' experience, a veteran lawkeeper, an officer of the Crown invested with as much authority as the Emperor himself, his eyes briefly widened with surprise. It was a minuscule opening, but Vonvalt saw it. Already he had the man on the back foot.

"This act," he continued loudly, "was witnessed by five-year-old Osgar Erikson. In an effort to ensure that word of his crime was not imparted, the boy was subsequently rendered insensible by Havener employing the Emperor's Voice. The boy passed into the care of the local abbey to have his complex, ongoing care needs met there, whilst Havener—asserts the Imperial Crown—made good his escape.

"With the assistance of his parents, Erikson was able to impart some scant details of the crime to the sheriff, but by that time, Vang had already been reported as having eloped with a Dennish deserter from the north, and in any event, the sheriff expired a short while later, and the matter was never resolved.

"A week ago, Justice Havener returned to Gdansburg to ensure—so the Imperial Crown asserts—that the boy remained more or less insensible, and to check that the body of Vang had not been uncovered from its resting place. In so doing, Sir Bronislav had miscalculated. The mere sight of the Justice was enough to stir the boy's residual memory of the horror he had witnessed, and he began to scream in terror. What is less clear is why the boy subsequently dropped dead. Well, I assert, on behalf of the Emperor, that Sir Bronislav did indeed slay the boy, using the same power that he had used to silence him in the first place. Children, the old, and the infirm, are uniquely susceptible to the power of the Emperor's Voice; it is perfectly possible to stop a person's heart in the right—" He looked pointedly at Havener. "—or indeed, the wrong circumstances."

Finally, the man snapped. "Enough of this!" he snarled. "Enough!"

"I shall come to you in a moment," Vonvalt said. "Ladies and gentlemen—"

"You will not ignore me!"

"I will gag you if I have to."

"I didn't murder anybody!"

"Still now you deny it?"

"I have never heard of Lissi Vang in my entire life. Where is your proof? Your *evidence*? I have enjoyed listening to your fable, Sir Konrad, but you cannot sentence me to anything without evidence. Every lawkeeper from Seaguard to the Frontier knows that."

"I have not called my witnesses yet. Be silent."

"A pox on your witnesses! They are going to add nothing to what you have already said, and these fucking dolts"—he gestured to the jury—"are going to call me guilty irrespective of anything and everything. None of this is impartial. None of this is proper. If you insist on trying me, return me to the capital, to the Magistratum. Everything else is a mistrial, and you know it."

"My dear Sir Bronislav, your knowledge of criminal procedure has returned! Miraculously! Here and now, where it serves you best!"

Havener tried to stand up, but his wrists were manacled to his legs. "False imprisonment," he grunted. "Beatings *in vinculis*. I would say that amounts to impermissible pre-trial torture. Arrest without charge. Detention without charge. Improper forensic procedure. An utterly partisan jury. These proceedings, and any conviction arising from them, are as safe as a groatwhore's cunt, and you know it."

Vonvalt's teeth were gritted so hard they threatened to buckle. What a viper this man was! Even the people of Gdansburg looked uncertain now, and Vonvalt's own uncertainty was compounding matters.

"I saw you," Vonvalt said. "I saw you through Osgar Erikson's eyes as you murdered that girl."

"And how is that?"

"I conducted a séance with her body."

"I do not think the jury heard you," Havener said caustically.

"I conducted a séance with her body."

Bressinger had been right. Vonvalt should have just killed him. He saw the looks of fear, unease, and even disgust on the faces around him. Necromancy provided evidence unrivalled in its probity, but the means to acquire it left people aghast and frightened, and as like to reject as to accept it. And now he had been forced to raise the matter on Havener's terms, rather than his own.

He looked at August, and she gave him a slight wince. Was he really this arrogant? Had he really let his time in Sova infect him with such egotism? Had he really thought he could half-arse his way through this, relying on the townsfolk's prejudice, however tacitly, to carry him over the line? To give the whole thing—a sham trial, truly—a veneer of legitimacy?

Vonvalt had one last course of action open to him.

"Where are your papers?" he asked.

"What?"

"Your effects? Your ledgers, your books, your judicial effects? Where are they?"

"I'm not answering any of your questions."

"Where are they?"

Havener looked around. Evidently he had expected the trial to be foreclosed after his tirade, and looked genuinely surprised that Vonvalt was continuing.

"I just told you, I'm not answering your questions."

"I have them."

Vonvalt—and just about everybody else in the town square—turned. Matria Klement was standing there, holding a volume.

"Fucking knew she was up to something," Bressinger muttered from the prosecutor's bench.

Klement advanced up the aisle between the standing public, clutching the volume as though her life depended on it.

Vonvalt turned part way to August and said, "My lady, I call Matria Radmila Klement as a witness for the prosecution."

"Thank you, Sir Konrad."

"Oh for Nema's sake," Havener spat. "What is this? Truly, what *is* this?"

"This, Justice, is your official journal from the 16th of Sorpen, 34 anno imperii Sovi," Klement said, holding it in front of her as though it were an illuminated manuscript.

"Where did you find that?" Havener snapped.

"Where you hid it."

Vonvalt looked at Bressinger, who shrugged.

"Preposterous!" Havener thundered.

Klement handed the volume to Vonvalt, who read the marked section. This was not at all where he had envisaged the trial going, but he was not about to look a gift horse in the mouth.

When he was finished, he handed the volume to August.

"Could you remind me, Sir Bronislav; you said you had never even heard of Lissi Vang?"

"I have not," Havener insisted, though he looked uneasy.

"It says here in your ledger that she came to you to make a criminal complaint on the 16th of Sorpen, Year 34. Do you recall writing this entry?"

"Will you not even let me look at it? You are obliged to, under evidentiary rules."

"I know what I am obliged to do," Vonvalt said. "I asked you a question."

"I have nothing to say."

Vonvalt took the ledger back from August, and read the entry. "L Vang approached with complaint of attempt at forced carnality. NFA." He snapped the ledger closed, making everybody start. "What does 'NFA' stand for, Sir Bronislav?"

The man remained silent.

"No further action," Vonvalt said. "Your entry. Your writing. Your signed and warranted ledger." He handed the volume to Havener, who did not even attempt to pick it up.

The man remained silent.

"What was the nature of the complaint she made to you, Sir Bronislav?"

Silence.

"Why did you not help her, Sir Bronislav?"

Silence.

"Why did she come to you, Justice Havener?!"

"Because I sent her!"

Vonvalt whirled around sharply, in time to see Klement collapsing to her knees, red-faced and trembling and weeping. "Because I sent her! Because he was supposed to help her and he didn't! She had a criminal complaint, and I sent her to the one person in the world who she should have been safe with, who she should have been able to depend on, to take her at her word! To investigate, and prosecute, and give her closure and justice! She never eloped!" Klement brandished a finger at Havener. "You murdered her!"

"For the last time, I did *not, drown,* Lissi *Vang*!" Havener thundered, spittle flying from his mouth, shouting with as much force as he could muster.

But instead of outcry and uproar and calamity, there was complete silence.

The cold ocean wind cut through the town square, and above, the sun made a brief appearance through the banks of autumnal cloud. Somewhere overhead, a marsh harrier cried out. The scent of ocean brine, and lunch, filled the air.

"What? What is it? What in Hell's name is the matter with all of you?"

Vonvalt sighed, and walked back over to the prosecutor's bench. "Sir Bronislav; how did you know she was drowned?"

Havener opened his mouth to speak, and then seemed to briefly choke, and then closed his mouth again. The silence persisted. Klement wept quietly in the aisle, and Mette knelt down on the dusty flagstones and embraced her and wept as well. Osgar's father began to walk towards Havener, but was smoothly intercepted by Bressinger.

"Let's take a walk, fella," Bressinger said, guiding the man away from the town square.

Vonvalt sat down heavily in his chair, and looked over to August. She nodded. "I think we shall leave matters there," she said quietly.

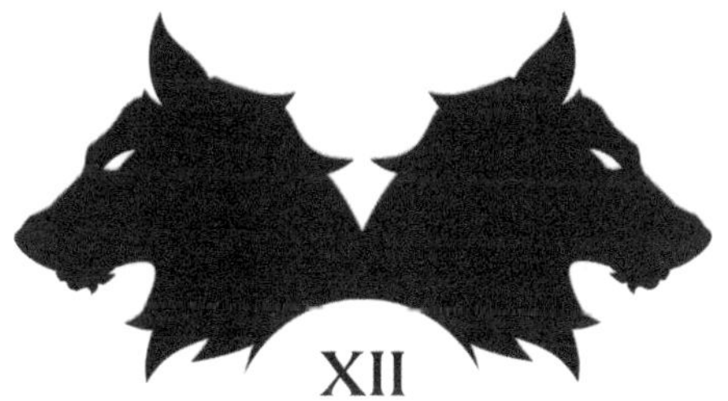

XII
THE DREGS OF REASON

"In the same way a bridge is made stronger with multiple supports, so must a Justice buttress their mind with the company and sympathetic ears of friends, colleagues, and associates. The legal profession is a burdensome one, placing, as it does, a great weight of human malfeasance on the shoulders of its enforcers. No lawkeeper can stew in these matters and not succumb to a melancholy affect; a Justice must therefore be careful to seize moments of levity, whenever and howsoever they are presented, with both hands."

—From Caterhauser's *The Sovan Criminal Code: Advice to Practitioners*

YOU WILL NOT tell me, even now?" Vonvalt asked.

Havener looked up, sallow and gaunt. He seemed as though he might expire simply of his own accord. Vonvalt had seen it; in the Sovan Legions, in his adolescence, men who could no longer take the privations of campaigning in the Reichskrieg. Men who simply… gave up.

"When am I scheduled to be executed?"

"This afternoon."

"What hour?"

"The second bell."

Havener nodded. Eventually, he said, "I was like you, once."

"How's that?"

"Young, and self-righteous, and so full of certainty and zeal."

"To the contrary, Sir Bronislav," Vonvalt murmured after a while. "I find myself plagued with self-doubt at every turn."

"Mm. You strike me as a thinking man," Havener said. It was not clear how it was meant, though it did not matter either way.

It was several days after the trial. In the sudden void of action left by Havener's accidental admission, Vonvalt had whisked him back to the gaol house and locked him inside, and then had drawn his sword, and August had drawn her sword, and together they had dissuaded the mob from lynching—well, all three of them, in the event. After several hours of inaction, and with blood and tempers cooled, Vonvalt had threatened them with illegal assembly, and that had put paid to any further attempts at vigilantism. The threat, however, had not truly passed until Osgar's father had bid everybody return to their homes, and let Imperial Justice run its course.

"It was nothing more than carnality. Old, tired lust," Havener said eventually. He stared at the straw decorating the cell floor. "She came to me, as Klement said. Had been *directed* to me. I suppose I feel guilty about that. On a different day, in different circumstances, I am certain I would have helped her—followed the thread of the case to its conclusion, prosecuted the wretch who had tried to force himself on her. Instead..." He shrugged. He looked up at Vonvalt briefly. "I didn't actually do anything to her."

"You mean, aside from murder her by drowning?"

Havener snorted bitterly. "Yes. Aside from that."

"And then there was the boy."

"And then there was the boy."

"And the sheriff."

Havener nodded before he had time to think about it. Then he chuckled, with only a hint of venom. "You little weasel." He shook his head. "You little rat."

Vonvalt shrugged. "Just lessening the paperwork. Why take it to your grave?"

"I shan't miss it. The administration, I mean."

Silence reclaimed the cell. Outside, Gdansburg went through the motions of a normal day.

Vonvalt sighed. "So you murdered her because… what? She could have undone your reputation?"

"She would have accused me of attempted rape."

Vonvalt arched an eyebrow. "Truthfully, in the event."

"Aye. No point in denying it now."

"No. Not now. What was it that caused you to act so wickedly?"

"I told you."

"Lust? Truly, that is it? Nothing more than an inability to control your base impulses?"

Havener simply shrugged.

"She came to you having come within a hairsbreadth of being forced to unwanted carnality, and you thought you would threaten her with the same?"

"I didn't *threaten* her with it, obviously," Havener snapped. "It was an invitation. It was just… Nema, it all sounds so absurd. So… malevolent, discussing it now."

"Because it *is*, Sir Bronislav. It *is* malevolent. These crimes… Any one of them would have been more than enough to send a man to the noose. To have committed all three, and all the ancillary offences that go with them, as a lawkeeper? As an officer of the Crown? As an Imperial *Justice*?"

"Oh, fuck off," Havener muttered. "Enough. I do not need you lecturing me on the evil nature of what it is I have done. I know full well the nature of it."

"And the boy? He was just in the wrong place at the wrong time?"

"Obviously."

Vonvalt shook his head. "Why did you come back? Why chance your arm so recklessly?"

"Sir Konrad, I've been asking myself the same question for the past week."

"You must have some notion."

"To see if anything had changed. To see if anything had been uncovered. To see if my crimes remained undetected. If I could come here, tour the town as part of my circuit, and not have a single person bat an eyelid, then I knew I could put the matter behind me. Move on. Relax slightly. It has been a burden on me for years, constantly at the back of my mind."

"If you are inviting me to furnish you with any sympathy whatever—"

"I am doing nothing of the sort. I am simply speaking my mind."

Vonvalt was quiet for a moment. "Would you like a confessor? You are entitled to one."

Havener smiled, and shook his head. "No thank you, Sir Konrad. I think you and I both know where I am headed."

"As you wish."

He stood there, hovering at the door.

"What? What is it?" Havener asked.

"It frightens me, honestly. That a man of your experience and standing could just throw it all away so recklessly. Without any thought. A life and a career extinguished in the course of an hour. Worse: to have caused so much anguish and heartache, and death. For no reason at all save to obfuscate your crime. It was all so…" Vonvalt threw his hands up helplessly. "Pointless. Needless. None of this need have happened. None of it whatsoever."

"And yet it has happened."

"And yet it has happened."

"Leave me. Let me prepare for death," Havener said, turning away.

Vonvalt left him.

OUTSIDE, BRESSINGER WAS loitering against the gaol house wall.

"What did he have to say for himself, then? You were in there longer than I thought you'd be."

Vonvalt didn't break his stride. "You were right."

"Right about what?"

"The answer to it all. The reasons. The explanation."

"Disappointing, was it?"

"It was nothing. Pointless. Death and misery thanks to the slightest increment of Fate's wheel. I should think that if Havener had spent ten minutes longer at his breakfast, none of it would have happened at all."

Bressinger watched his master sweep on through the town, and leant back against the wall, and took no satisfaction whatever in being right.

HAVENER WAS A Justice, not a commoner, and so was entitled to the sword by law.

"I say we drag him over to that marsh and drown him," Bressinger said. He had donned, as was required of him, his formal black cloak ahead of the execution. Vonvalt and August had done the same. "See how he likes it."

Vonvalt had ordered a scaffold constructed, and then had allowed Mette, Erik, and Freya to speak. Their powerful, harrowing testimony had left the crowd feeling charged with rage once more, but it was their right, and an important part of the retributive aspect of the judicial process. There was no rehabilitating Havener, after all.

It was a sunny afternoon, and a warm breeze blew through the town square. Havener was brought out, and forced to his knees on the scaffold. Bressinger bent down and gathered up the man's hair, and pulled it out of the way, stretching his neck over the chopping block.

"Justice Sir Bronislav Havener," Vonvalt said in a loud, clear voice. "You have confessed to murdering Ms Lissi Vang, Master Osgar Erikson, and Sheriff Vilhelm Lund, in the month of Sorpen, thirty-four anno imperii Sovi. By His Most Excellent Majesty, the Emperor Kzosic IV, I, His Justice, Sir Konrad Vonvalt, do adjudge you guilty, and sentence you to die by beheading. Do you have anything to say?"

"Only that I regret it," Havener replied.

Vonvalt drew his short sword. Now Havener began to shake and whimper. "Get it done!" he gasped.

Vonvalt brought the sword down and severed the man's head cleanly, and Bressinger pulled it away and free. Next to them, August noted down the date and time in her ledger. The crowd of Gdansburgers cheered and celebrated, though plenty looked unhappy, as was common, in Vonvalt's experience, even where the condemned was widely hated.

"That's done then," Vonvalt said. He ran a rag down the length of his blade, and then sheathed it. He looked over to the abbey. "One final thing. Then we can leave this place."

"I'M NOT INTERRUPTING anything, am I?" he asked as he entered Matria Klement's office. She looked up at him briefly, and then returned to packing her belongings.

"I wondered how long it would be before you came to see me."

"I had expected to see you at the execution."

"I am just too tired of that man to bestir myself to watch his death. I take no satisfaction in any of it anymore."

Vonvalt nodded. "I know that feeling."

She continued to pack, and it was clear from the nature of the things she was taking—trinkets, personal effects—that she was quitting Gdansburg for good.

"You feel guilt, I imagine," he said eventually.

"I sent that girl to her death."

"Unwittingly."

"It makes no difference. She would not have done it without my recommendation."

"There was a Dennish deserter, then?"

"Aye."

"What happened to him?"

"Truly, I know not."

Vonvalt examined the office. "Why did you not tell me everything you knew? Straight away?"

"You know why. I have said it directly to you often enough."

Vonvalt nodded. "I suppose so."

"What is there to suppose? You would have let him go."

"I would not have."

"Perhaps not you personally. But could you say the same for every other Imperial Magistrate passing through this way? What if the man, or woman, had been a contemporary of Havener's? I can tell you are significantly younger than him. Perhaps even a generation apart. What if one of his friends had come?"

"There is no use speculating."

"And yet I have speculated. And I do not like where my speculation takes me."

"What is the point in questioning what might have been? It wasn't another Justice. It was me. And now Havener is dead, like you wanted."

"You think I should be pleased with all this?"

"I think you should be pleased that I am not prosecuting you for extrajudicial murder."

"Do you really think these rules and procedures and the Imperial common law amount to anything?"

"It is not a question of what I think. The reality of these matters is patent."

She did not answer. Instead, she finished packing her bags, and then, to Vonvalt's surprise, donned maille and a white surcoat, and affixed around her waist a Sovan short sword, and strapped across her back a sohle shield.

"You mean to return to the Frontier?"

"I shall go back to Südenburg, aye," she said. "And make my penance there."

"What do you have to atone for?"

"If you think I can stay here, you are a fool. I am the author of everyone's misfortune."

"Justice Havener is that."

Again, she did not answer. Instead she pushed past him, a diminutive old woman sagging under the weight of her decades-old armour. She lifted a dented kettle helm off the back of the office door, and left.

Vonvalt never saw her again—but then, he did not expect to.

EPILOGUE

POLITICAL ANIMALS

"The Magistratum interprets and applies the law, but the Emperor and the Senate create it. The former draws its authority from the latter, and the wise Justice keeps a weather eye on the vicissitudes of the Imperial Household."

—From Caterhauser's *The Sovan Criminal Code: Advice to Practitioners*

THEY RETURNED TO Sova.

The journey took the better part of a month. They passed great work gangs building the western limb of the Imperial Relay—what would become a large paved high-way running from the top of the Empire to its westernmost tip. Every ten miles or so was a staging station, where Imperial officials could switch out exhausted horses for a fresh set and so cover a tremendous amount of ground in a short space of time. But the high-way had not yet been finished, and they had to take the old Grozodan dirt roads across the countryside.

Autumn was waning by the time they reached the vast Imperial capital. They entered via the Creus Gate and then turned south down the Veleurian Road. Here, between the high-way and the western branch of the turbid River Sauber stood the Grand Lodge, home of the Magistratum. It was a huge building, mostly formed of a single square tower several hundred feet high, itself sitting on a large box of white stone honeycombed with lodgings and legal chambers. At the top of the tower was a two-headed wolf colossus. Written on the side of the tower, rendered in black iron lettering, was:

NO ONE IS ABOVE THE LAW

"Not even Justices," Vonvalt murmured as he dismounted.

"What's that?" Bressinger asked.

"Nothing. See that our horses are stabled. Then you had might as well do what you will. I think this will take some time."

"Suits me."

"Come and find me tomorrow."

Vonvalt looked up at the colossus high above. "Come on then," he said to August. "Let's get this over with."

MASTER KRUGER WAS the seniormost Justice in the Order and the Empire's Legal Prefect, and received them in his chamber. It was an ostentatious office overlooking the city of Sova, and Kruger occupied a thronelike armchair behind an enormous desk of polished wood with an inlaid leather surface covered in a career's worth of *objets*.

"Justices Vonvalt and August," Kruger said. He was a large, thickset man, hirsute and greying though he was only ten years Vonvalt's senior. He had a naturally displeased expression, though he might have been displeased to see Vonvalt anyway. The latter enjoyed such prominence within Sova's corridors of power that he was frequently mooted as

Kruger's successor. "To what do I owe the pleasure? I did not think you, Sir Konrad, were due back in Sova for the better part of a year."

"I'm afraid I bring bad news with me to the capital—the sort of news I think best delivered in person."

"Is that so?"

"'Tis, my lord."

"All right then. Let's have it."

Vonvalt explained what had taken place in Gdansburg. He spoke for half an hour. August offered her corroboration wherever she could. Kruger listened more or less in silence, asking the odd question, but otherwise letting them speak. By the time Vonvalt had finished, the sun was low in the sky, and the weather was closing in.

"Bloody hell," Kruger muttered, standing. He turned to look out the window, clasping his hands behind his back. "I suppose there's no use in asking whether you could have made any sort of mistake?"

Vonvalt shook his head. "He confessed it all, in the end."

After a little while, Kruger turned and rummaged around in his desk drawers, and pulled out a bottle of brandy and several crystal tumblers. He poured three large measures, and Vonvalt gratefully accepted his, though August demurred.

"What did you do with the body?"

"Burnt on a convict's pyre."

"Did you at least give him the sword?"

"As per procedure, aye,"

"Well, you say 'as per procedure', Konrad, but it seems to me you have done almost everything but."

August stirred. "I counselled Sir Konrad to hold as best a version of a criminal trial as we could, as a—"

"Propaganda exercise, yes, I grasp it all perfectly," Kruger muttered. "Gods, couldn't the two of you have just brought him back here? Or killed him quietly? Why put on a bloody great show trial?"

Vonvalt's brow furrowed. "I thought it important, Master, to demonstrate that not even an Imperial Magistrate is above the law."

"You thought that important, did you?"

"Was I mistaken?"

Kruger regarded him for a few moments. "What are we, Sir Konrad?"

"Magistrates, Master."

"What do we do?"

"Enforce the Sovan common law. Both criminal and civil."

"Where?"

"The Empire—"

"The *Em*pire, verily!" Kruger snapped. "These are Imperial subjects, man. And we are Imperial officers, first and foremost. We do not spend time and effort—we *certainly* do not spend Justice's lives—to indulge the commonfolk. You should have brought him back here."

"Justice Havener is governed by the same rules as everyone—"

"Don't be so bloody stupid!" the man erupted. "We are *political* animals, Konrad. We are not merely arbiters of the common law. We are extensions of Sova. We must be seen to be infallible. Bulwarks of civilisation. We are representatives of the nation state. The iron fist of House Haugenate! You do not kowtow to the demands of the mob. To provincials. To bandits and vigilantes. What have you done except *erode* faith in the Magistratum? In Sova? That her very own legal officers could commit—*Nema!*—a near full house of capital crimes?"

Vonvalt had weathered a great many diatribes from a great many powerful men and women, and so he weathered this one. But there was something about being told so directly, so plainly, about such systemic malfeasance that shocked him. Worse, that he was expected to be complicit in it.

"Will that be all, Master?" Vonvalt asked, making to stand. August looked briefly wide-eyed at his insouciance.

"Will that be all? Are you fucking serious?"

"Honestly, Master, I'm not quite sure what more there is to be gained by continuing the conversation."

"This is not a *conversation*, Konrad," Kruger said, astonished. "This is a bollocking. This is a dressing-down. There will be a disciplinary hearing. Your Royal warrant will be suspended. Your practice licence will be revoked. Am I making myself clear? You *killed* another Justice, Konrad. Put him down like a dog." He made an incredulous noise. "I can't think of a single precedent for this."

Vonvalt nodded calmly. He took his medallion off, and placed it on the desk, and then he withdrew his warrant, which was kept in a leather wallet, and his seal, and placed them both on the desk as well. "Have the clerks notify me of the hearing, Master, and I shall present my person."

Kruger trembled with anger. "Get out of here, the pair of you, before I have you whipped!"

✦

"ARE YOU QUITE bloody mad?" August asked as they made their way back through the Magistratum. "He's going to disbar you."

"No, he isn't," Vonvalt said, his features downturned in disgust. "My effects will be returned to me tomorrow, and no further action will be taken."

August snorted in disbelief. Vonvalt watched out the corner of his eye as she examined him. "How is it that you are so self-possessed? Truly? What is this elixir of confidence that you have consumed? You are always so certain of matters."

"He said it himself. If we are political animals, embodiments of the Sovan state, then why would we expose ourselves so politically? Why would we give our enemies such an easy opportunity to attack us? What is he going to do? Try me? Put me through some sort of disciplinary hearing? It's nonsense. He's just angry that I did what he would not. If it were up to him, Havener would be back here, working as a Jurist for a year or two, before being turned loose out on circuit again."

"You really think that?"

"I'm certain of it."

They exited the Grand Lodge and out on to the Veleurian Road. The cold wind was picking up. It reminded Vonvalt of Gdansburg.

"What's the lesson in all this?" August asked after a while.

"That perhaps the Magistratum is not quite as good at stamping out our humanity as it likes to think it is."

"I don't like this side of you. I think I preferred it when you were more of an idealist."

"I am an idealist."

"Hm."

They stopped at the Creus Road junction and stood there in front of the enormous Temple of Nema.

"What will you do now?"

"Knock about the capital for a few days. Wait for Kruger to give me my things back. And then I shall go back to work."

"Do you want to get dinner first?"

"I'd love to."

"Will you stay with me tonight?"

"I'd love that, too."

"Come on then," August said, putting her arm through his, and they went to find somewhere to eat.

"PACKAGE FOR YOU," Bressinger said as he entered Vonvalt's chambers the next day, dropping a cloth parcel on his desk.

Vonvalt sniffed the air around his taskman. "You smell like a brothel."

"Cock's back to normal, ain't it."

"Delightful."

"I think it was the peat, you know."

Vonvalt ignored him, and opened the parcel. Inside was his warrant, seal, and medallion.

"What's the story there?" Bressinger asked, pointing his chin at the contents.

"Nothing," Vonvalt sighed.

"What's next?"

"We have much work to do."

"You always say that."

"You are free to leave my service at any time."

Bressinger shook his head. "Pay's too good."

Vonvalt stood, and put his medallion on, and pocketed his warrant and seal. Then he lifted his waxed cloak from its hook on the back of the door, and picked up a volume of precedent from his desk.

"Come, then," he said, sweeping towards the door. "Let us be about it."

ACKNOWLEDGMENTS

This novella would not exist in any form without Adrian Collins, Editor-in-Chief at *Grimdark Magazine*, and my sincerest thanks go to him for suggesting, commissioning, managing, administrating, beautifying (and just about everything-ing this novella short of writing it) *The Scour*.

Thanks also to Ed Crocker for his editorial efforts, René Aigner for the cover, Shawn King for design services, Jack Shepherd for the map, Matt Holland at the Broken Binding for his support, and Bronte-Marie Wesson for letting me use the name 'Brass Wyvern'—I'm tremendously grateful to you all.

www.ingramcontent.com/pod-product-compliance
Lightning Source LLC
Chambersburg PA
CBHW020611310726
48979CB00008B/1440/J
9781923459021